MOONLIGHT KISSES

Devon drained h n the empty champagne b. He reached out both h

"How could you rable unless you auditione e dim moonlight, Phillipa could just make out the devilish glint in his eyes.

Feeling wickedly mischievous herself and not thinking beyond the moment, Phillipa said, "I concede your point, my lord," stood up, and stepped into his extended arms.

Devon wound his hands around Phillipa's waist and pulled her close. She rested her hands on the curve of his broad shoulders and tilted her face up toward his. Her heart began to beat a little faster.

Devon lowered his head, placed his mouth onto hers, and caressed her lips in a sweet, languid kiss and stepped back.

"How was it?"

Phillipa breathed a sigh. "I have had better," she lied. The pressure of his mouth had shaken her to her toes as Cedric's carefully chaste kisses had never done.

Fibber. Devon smiled to himself. The lady had trembled in his arms when his lips had touched hers. She had felt the beginnings of the flare of heat as much as he had. *Had better, eh? We'll just see about that . . .*

From A PICTURE PERFECT ROMANCE
by Alice Holden

<u>BOOK YOUR PLACE ON OUR WEBSITE</u> <u>AND MAKE THE</u> <u>READING CONNECTION!</u>

We've created a customized website just for our very special readers, where you can get the inside scoop on everything that's going on with Zebra, Pinnacle and Kensington books.

When you come online, you'll have the exciting opportunity to:

- View covers of upcoming books
- Read sample chapters
- Learn about our future publishing schedule (listed by publication month *and author*)
- Find out when your favorite authors will be visiting a city near you
- Search for and order backlist books from our online catalog
- Check out author bios and background information
- Send e-mail to your favorite authors
- Meet the Kensington staff online
- Join us in weekly chats with authors, readers and other guests
- Get writing guidelines
- AND MUCH MORE!

Visit our website at
http://www.zebrabooks.com

HIS BLUSHING BRIDE

Elena Greene
Alice Holden
Regina Scott

ZEBRA BOOKS
Kensington Publishing Corp.
http://www.zebrabooks.com

CONTENTS

Dear Linette

Happy reading!

THE WEDDING WAGER

Elena Greene

Elena M. Greene
5/26/01

One

"Harriet! You're not supposed to laugh when a gentleman proposes marriage."

"I'm sorry, Julian. I can't help it; it is too absurd. You must be bosky!" Harry Woodford quelled her laughter and eyed her friend curiously.

Julian had dined with them informally, as he often did while in Kent. He'd only had several glasses of wine with dinner, and he and Papa had not spent much time over their port before rejoining her and Aunt Claudia in their cozy drawing room. Harry also knew that despite his growing reputation as a rake, Julian really didn't drink more than most men. Still, she couldn't think of another reason why he would propose to her.

"I'm not the slightest bit foxed," he insisted, indignation lighting his vivid blue eyes. "I am perfectly serious. Will you marry me?"

"No. I still cannot believe you are asking me. You must be drunk, but don't worry," she said in a soothing tone. "I promise to forget what you've said by tomorrow morning."

"I tell you I'm sober as a judge!" he shouted. Harry winced, then looked toward the other end of the room to see if Papa or Aunt Claudia had noticed. Papa looked up from his sporting periodical and gave them a brief, indulgent smile before resuming his reading. Aunt Claudia had fallen asleep over her embroidery, lulled by the warmth of their fire and the sound of a late March rainstorm tapping against the windows.

Then Harriet looked back at Julian. He certainly didn't *look* as if he were in his cups, she thought, now thoroughly baffled.

"Don't you see?" he asked, in a slightly calmer tone. "This is an excellent notion, one of the best I've ever had."

"That's precisely what I *don't* see," she replied. "What is this all about? Are you in debt?"

"No, of course not. What do you think, that I'm some sort of fortune-hunter, after your Papa's money? You ought to know better!"

His look of indignation deepened into outrage, and Harry realized she'd spoken impulsively. It didn't make sense that Julian would need her fortune; he owned a large estate bordering the Woodfords' own Kentish estate, and received a very generous allowance from his trustees. Besides, it wasn't gambling, any more than drinking, that had gained Julian his notoriety.

"I'm sorry," she said. "I spoke without thinking."

He smiled, and Harriet relaxed. Julian never could stay angry for long.

"If you aren't in debt, what is it?" she asked.

"I suppose I should explain," he said, running a hand through his fair hair. It was a sure sign that he was embarrassed. "It's my uncles," he continued, and then stopped as if carefully choosing his next words.

"Oh, I see," she interrupted. "Do you think they will agree to end the trust if you marry?"

"Well, yes," he replied, looking relieved at her ready grasp of his situation. "You do understand, don't you?"

Harry nodded. Few persons understood Julian's circumstances as well as she did.

He had become the fifth Viscount Debenham at the tender age of five years old. Since that time, his uncles had acted as both his guardians and his trustees; they held the right to control both Julian's estate and the considerable Ardleigh fortune until he reached the age of thirty, or such time that they deemed him mature enough to take on the responsibility himself. Unfortunately, the two overzealous old gentlemen still treated Julian as if he were the small, lonely boy they had taken charge of twenty years ago.

Julian usually made light of the situation; only his closest friends, including Harriet, knew how it irked him to hold the title but not be allowed any part in the management of the estate. No doubt his proposal sprang from a desire to impress his uncles with his maturity. Though married, neither of his uncles had any children. Morbidly anxious about the succession, they had been plaguing Julian to marry and set up his nursery ever since he had left Cambridge.

"You're not offended, are you?"

Julian's anxious words pulled Harry out of her reverie.

"No," she said with a smile. "Although perhaps I should be. I'm sorry, but I still think the notion of our marrying is preposterous."

"Don't you think we'd suit? We've been friends forever," he retorted.

It was perfectly true. The Ardleigh and Woodford lands marched together for miles, and as children, Julian and Harry had happily explored every inch of them together. But, Harry thought a little wistfully, they were no longer children. If Julian hadn't realized that they had also grown apart a little, she did.

"For that very reason, perhaps," she replied. "Besides, I haven't the slightest wish to marry. Surely you've met plenty of other ladies who would suit you much better than I would."

"There's no one I care for more than you."

She looked down. There was a warmth in his voice, but she knew it for what it was: mere fondness for a childhood friend. "You need someone who will enter into all of your interests," she argued. "You know how I hate London, and I despise fashionable parties. I was obliged to endure all that five years ago, during my one Season. I'm not about to suffer through it all again, not for anything!"

"You know, Harry, you really should give London another try. If we married, I'd introduce you to all my friends, take you to parties, the theatre. It would do you good."

"Please stop!" she said, exasperated. "There's no use discussing it any further. I'm perfectly content where I am. I have my horses, and my dogs, and no one tells me what to do, not even Papa."

"What, do you think I'd be some sort of Bluebeard?"

"No, I know you would never be unkind. But why me? I'm sure there are dozens of young ladies who would give their souls to become the next Viscountess Debenham." Pretty ones, too, Harry thought silently. The sort men really *wanted* to marry, not plain, mousy-haired, gray-eyed hoydens who preferred riding to flirtation.

"Yes, but that's the problem," said Julian. "How do I know any of those ladies wouldn't marry me if I were fifty years old and ugly as sin?"

"I don't wish to pander to your vanity," she replied. "But I'm sure there are any number of them mooning their hearts out over you, and you know it."

Julian reddened. Clearly he was not unaware of the effect his outrageously good looks and sweet manner had on most women. "But I don't care for any of them the way I care for *you*. And the devil of it is, most of 'em bore me to death after a few dances. You don't bore me."

"That's a ludicrous reason to marry. Besides, I know for a fact that not *all* the women in London bore you to death," she said with a mischievous smile.

"What do you know about it? You shouldn't listen to gossip."

"I don't—you told me yourself! When you first went to London, there was that blonde opera dancer that almost ruined you with her demands for expensive jewelry. Then there was that young widowed marchioness, then—"

"Did I tell you all that?" he asked, his color deepening. "What was I thinking?"

"Don't worry, I'm not judging you. I'm sure none of your ladybirds have ever complained of how you treated them. But I'll have you know I won't marry a philanderer."

"Oh, I would give all that up once we marry," he promised.

She laughed at his blithe tone. "I know you. You can never resist a pretty face, or a well-turned ankle. You've said so yourself."

"If I did, I was just joking. I could be faithful, if I needed to be. Give me credit for *some* resolution."

"Not where most women are concerned. You wouldn't last three months!"

"Oh yes I would."

"No, you wouldn't. You couldn't."

"I tell you I could."

Harry had seen that stubborn look in Julian's eyes before. Once he took a notion into his head, it was almost impossible to get it out again, except by the utmost force. She had best think of something, or he would plague her about it for months.

"Very well, then," she said. "I propose a wager."

"A wager?" he asked, looking surprised.

"A wager. If you can refrain from so much as kissing another woman for the next three months, I will marry you."

Julian stared at her for a few moments, then a broad smile blazed across his face as he answered, "I accept!"

"Wait," she said, holding up her hand. "You haven't heard my other conditions."

"Well, what are they?"

"First, if you fail—"

"I won't!"

"If you fail, I get Titania's next foal."

"That's easy. 'With all my worldly goods I thee endow'—isn't that what the vows say? If I win, you get *all* my horses."

The entrancing prospect of combining horse-breeding operations with Julian took temporary possession of Harry's imagination. Then she mentally shook herself; of all the reasons for her and Julian to marry, it had to be the most insane.

Thinking quickly, she stated her remaining conditions. "You will go back to London next week as you planned, and continue all your usual social engagements during the Season. You will *not* tell anyone of our wager. No one must even suspect that you have offered for me."

"That sounds fair. But how am I going to prove that I won if you're not around to see it? I don't want you to accuse me of cheating."

"I would never do that. I know you wouldn't lie to me. Just come and visit us once a week—say, every Tuesday—and tell me how you are faring."

"Very well, I accept the wager," he said. "We will be married by the end of June. You had best start ordering your bride-clothes!"

She shook her head, smiling. "My dear friend, you don't stand a chance."

TWO

Julian whistled as he trod over the threshold of the elegant lodging in Park Street. He had just returned to London; this evening, he would attempt to clear the first obstacle toward winning Harriet's hand. It might be a rasper, but he'd taken precautions to make sure he didn't come to grief.

Conducted by a maid to a lady's boudoir, decorated in shades of blush and cream, Julian was instantly aware of the beguiling scent of roses. He beheld the equally familiar but pleasant sight of his mistress, Annette Fauré, reclining on a sofa.

"*Mon cher* Julian!" she trilled. "I 'ave meesed you so zees last week!" She jumped up from the sofa and ran to greet him, dark curls bobbing; the ribbons on her frilly dressing-gown fluttered in her haste. In another instant, her fragrant, soft shape was pressed up against him and an equally soft rosebud of a mouth sought his.

"Hello, Annette," he said, hastily turning his head aside. Good Lord, he'd almost lost the bet already! Or would it not count against him if he didn't kiss back? He decided it was better not to pursue that line of thought.

"Julian! What is it? Do you not love your faithful

Annette anymore? Can you not see 'ow I have been pining away in your absence?"

From the bloom in her cheeks, it didn't look as if she were pining away, but that didn't make Julian any more comfortable, not with her delicious form pressed up against his. Gently, he removed her arms from his waist and was gratified to find that this was easier to do than he had expected. He led her back to the sofa and sat her down. Then he took his seat at the other end, at what was hopefully a safe distance.

She gazed at him with melting, pansy-brown eyes. He hoped she wasn't going to make this difficult.

"I have a present for you, Annette. I hope you will like it," he said, pulling a small jewelry case from his pocket.

She gave him a quick look from under her long eyelashes, then took the case from him. She opened it up and examined the ruby and diamond brooch twinkling up at her.

"It is lovely, *mon amour.* You must allow me to thank you for such a wonderful gift," she said, sliding closer toward him.

"Er, that won't be necessary," he said, edging away.

"Ah, I understand now," she said, mournfully. "It is to say good-bye, is it not?"

"Yes, darling, I'm afraid it is. And to thank you for so many happy times."

"I knew it!" she said in a low, ominous voice.

Julian tensed. Annette had never enacted a scene for him before. She'd always been the merriest of companions; almost perfect, in fact, except for her tiresome French accent. He knew for a fact that her real name was Annie Forrest, and she'd never even been to Dover, let alone to France. He would also have sworn that her sensibilities were as little engaged as his.

"Julian! 'Ow can you do zis? Cast me off—abandon *moi,* a poor, defenseless woman, to a cold, cruel world!" She covered her face with her hands.

Egad! She seemed about to break into tears. If there was anything Julian couldn't bear, it was to see a woman cry. Unfortunately, the best way he knew to make it stop was to kiss her, and that was clearly out of the question.

"I'm sorry," he said, clumsily patting her shoulder. "But there are circumstances. I thought you always knew this would not last forever."

"Deserter! Villain! You are breaking my heart!" she said with a sob, her soft, rounded white shoulders shaking.

It was hopeless. There was nothing for it but to take her into his arms. Surely a gallant hug was not a violation of his wager.

"Please don't cry!" he said, stroking her back. "You know how fond I am of you. But, really, I cannot—"

She lifted her face, and Julian was thunderstruck to see her giggling.

"Oh, Julian darling!" she said, with an abrupt loss of her assumed French accent. "When I saw how solemn you were, I couldn't resist playing with you just a trifle."

"A dashed nasty trick to play," he said, laughing at himself now. "You really had me worried!"

"Oh, I am truly sorry. But you need not worry about me. I shall be brave, I shall hide my despair under a laughing face, and hope that in time my heart will mend!" she said, resuming her earlier manner and rolling her eyes theatrically.

"Will you stop it at once!" he protested, hastily releasing her from his embrace and moving back to his earlier position. "You will do very well indeed. Now that I come to think of it, the Marquess of Weststoke was most taken with you at that little party we held in Leicestershire. I was pretty sure at the time he wanted to lure you away from me."

"Oh, Lord Weststoke is most charming, but of course there will never be anyone quite like you, my *galant* Julian." He read confirmation of his suspicions in her face, in her half-mischievous, half-guilty expression. She would be under Weststoke's protection within the fortnight or Julian would eat his best chapeau bras.

"But you must tell why you are leaving me now, Julian. I hope it is not that I have bored you, *mon cher?*" she said, looking worried.

Oh Lord! He'd promised Harry not to tell anyone of their wager. But he didn't have the heart to tell Annie he'd tired of her. Even if, as he suddenly realized, it was true.

"No, it's not that, it's just—"

"Ah, are you going to be married?" she asked, looking at him shrewdly. "How very romantic, to be sure!"

Julian realized he wouldn't be able to deny it. However, he hadn't lost the wager—not yet. Harry had stipulated that he couldn't tell anyone, and he hadn't. Annette had guessed on her own.

"Don't tell anyone, please," he said. "It's of the utmost importance."

"You know you can trust me to be discreet," she said with a reassuring smile. "So, tell me about this new bride of yours. Who is she? I hope she is very pretty and amusing."

He thought of Harry, and decided he didn't want to discuss her with Annette.

"I'm sorry, I must be leaving now," he answered shortly, getting to his feet.

"But why hurry away, *mon cher?*" she asked, jumping to her feet and rushing to block his exit. "Surely you can stay just a little longer? You are not yet married, and you know I shall miss you. Why can we not enjoy one more evening together?"

"I must go," he insisted.

"But I have not yet thanked you for your gift!" she sighed, swaying toward him as he stood in the middle of her delicately patterned carpet. Her rose-scent wafted up to him, and he couldn't help remembering how much Annie enjoyed her work. An inner voice urged Julian to put his arms around that slim waist just one more time, but at the same time, another voice—a surprisingly strong one, too—told him he'd regret it if he did.

"Good-bye, Annie," he said firmly, after a short struggle.

"Then just one last kiss!" She flung her arms around his neck and lifted her face to him, puckering her full, plummy lips. "What harm could there be in one last kiss?"

"More than you know!" he answered, chuckling. This time he had no trouble at all silencing the impish voice of temptation.

He lifted her up, set her gently to one side, and left. Safely outside the door of her lodging, he exhaled a deep sigh of relief.

He'd done it. He'd met what was probably the most difficult challenge of his wager with Harriet. From now on, it was sure to be smooth sailing.

* * *

Over the next week, Julian successfully avoided a variety of temptations.

A few of his friends were in town already. So, true to his agreement with Harriet, he accepted a friend's invitation to a masculine party. However, he was a bit taken aback to discover that his friend, having had a recent streak of luck at the gaming tables, had provided not only the usual wine and cards as entertainment, but had also hired a few Cyprians to liven up the occasion.

Somehow, Julian managed to flirt lightly with the buxom charmer who singled him out for her attentions. He did so until his host and the other guests were either three parts drunk or had wandered off with their own chosen ladybirds. Then he handed her a handsome largesse for her trouble, and slipped quietly away.

Later in the week, he attended Lady Brandon's ball, one of the first of the Season. Lady Brandon was good-natured and hospitable, and he knew she had been a friend of his mother's. He didn't have the heart to refuse her invitation, particularly since she knew he was in town. Besides, he'd promised Harry.

Once there, he couldn't help but dance with any number of pleasant young ladies. Unlike some young bucks, he couldn't offend his kind hostess or her fair guests by brooding about in a corner in an attempt to look rakish, or by refusing to dance anything but waltzes. Truth be told, he actually enjoyed the lively rhythm of country dances. At present, they were also much safer than the more intimate waltz, although he couldn't avoid that, either.

He did manage to gracefully turn down suggestions by several of his partners that they might enjoy a turn on the terrace. Pretty as some of the young ladies were, he knew better than to indulge them. He wouldn't still be a bachelor at the age of five and twenty if he hadn't learned to avoid such potentially compromising situations.

As he'd promised, he visited Harry on the following Tuesday. They spent a pleasant day out of doors. However, when he told her how easily he was passing her test, she only laughed at him, saying it was early days to be foretelling victory. Julian returned to London doubly determined to prove her wrong.

The next week passed in much the same manner, and the following one as well. Harry spent her time as usual, helping her father run their estate, including the stud farm that was their pride and joy. She enjoyed Julian's visits, particularly since she usually did not see so much of him during the London Season.

She also observed him closely, looking for early signs of strain from his self-imposed celibacy. It could be only a matter of time, surely, before he succumbed to temptation. However, she rather hoped it wouldn't happen too soon. She didn't want to admit it, but she would miss his visits.

Harriet steadied the chestnut mare around the turn as they approached the makeshift fence at the far end of the paddock. Out of the corner of her eye, she saw another horse and rider coming down the nearby ride. It was Julian, and he was early.

She turned her attention back toward the upcoming jump; too late, for Circe sensed her lapse of concentration. Harry flew over the fence; unfortunately, the mare remained on the other side.

Annoyed but unhurt, Harry sprang back to her feet and dusted off the skirt of her riding habit. How had she allowed Julian to distract her so? At least she had managed to hold onto the reins; she didn't need Julian teasing her about *that* as well as her ignominious tumble.

"You little witch!" she said sternly as she came around the fence toward the horse, who was waiting on the opposite side of the fence with an expression of spurious equine innocence. As Harry reached the mare, she heard Julian call out.

"Harry, I thought I taught you better!"

"You distracted me," she retorted, watching him ride up to the paddock gate on his tall roan. "To be sure, it is my own fault for not concentrating."

She remounted, and urged Circe back into a canter. Heading toward the fence again, she put all other thoughts aside. She knew she had to ride with supreme confidence, or Circe would sense her ambivalence and refuse again.

This time they cleared the fence in perfect form.

"What a nice little mare you have there," said Julian, applauding.

"Yes, but it is the greatest shame that she can't be trusted for one instant. I fear I shall never succeed in transforming her into a reliable mount."

"Don't be so distrustful! Don't you know anyone is capable of improvement, from a horse to a confirmed rake?" he asked, grinning.

His smile was dangerously charming. If Harry didn't know better, she might start imagining his efforts at reformation were on her account. Or that he would succeed.

"It's a little early to be crowing victory," she said.

"You don't think I can stay the course, do you? Well, I'll prove you wrong."

"We shall see," she replied amicably. She wasn't surprised Julian had managed to hold out thus far. Surely it was too early to worry. There were still nine long weeks to go before their bet would run its course. Nine weeks full of gaiety and temptations. Plenty of time for some lady to lure him into dalliance, thought Harry, with a surprising tinge of regret. Of course, when the bet was over, she would see less of Julian. She had best enjoy their time together while it lasted.

"Shall we go for a ride?" she asked, to change the subject. "There's a young bay I think you might like to try."

Julian agreed, and they set off toward the stables so that their tired mounts could be properly cared for. A quarter of an hour later, they had set off down the lane, Julian mounted on the bay hunter prospect, Harry on a young dappled gray gelding.

"He's a pretty thing, ain't he?" Julian commented, looking at Harry's horse. "A bit showy for a hunter, but he looks sound enough."

"Troubadour is a sweet fellow," she said, fondly patting the horse's velvety shoulder. "He should make some lady a fine hack. I'm just putting the finishing touches on his education."

"Do you have a buyer in mind?"

"Lady Dearing is interested. She is looking for a handsome mount to ride in the parks."

Harry eyed Julian curiously. Lady Dearing was a wealthy widow, exactly the sort of woman he favored. She might not be in the absolute first blush of youth; however, her golden good looks, opulent figure, and lack of a jealous husband should make her an ideal partner for a carefree young buck like Julian.

"I'm sure she'll be quite pleased with Troubadour," Julian answered, seeming quite unconscious.

For some reason, Harry couldn't resist probing further. "Do you know Lady Dearing?"

He looked at her shrewdly before replying. "Yes, but not in the biblical sense, if that's what you're thinking! I've met her at a few parties, but our paths have never really crossed."

She must have looked doubtful, for he continued, "I'll admit she's a charming woman, but as you know quite well, I'm finished with all that. I don't even miss it."

She couldn't help giggling at his virtuous look. Nevertheless, she was rather relieved that he hadn't had an *affaire* with Lady Dearing. Which was perfectly silly. Of course he'd had plenty of liaisons with other ladies that Harry hadn't met.

"Don't laugh at me, Harry!" said Julian, recalling her attention. "If you and your aunt will only come up to London, you'll see how well I can avoid temptation."

"I'm sure I can trust you to tell me when you finally succumb. There's no need for me to go to London."

She saw Julian eyeing her curiously. She hoped he wasn't going to ask about her aversion to London. The winter preceding Harry's first Season, Julian had taken a bad fall while fox-hunting. He'd spent the next few months languishing in Leicestershire while his broken ribs and other injuries healed. When they'd seen each other again, she had been disinclined to discuss what had happened, and fortunately he hadn't pried. It seemed she wasn't so lucky now.

"I've heard rumors, but I wish you will tell me yourself what happened that Season. Why do you despise

London so much?" he asked, in a gentle tone that was difficult to resist.

She frowned. "I didn't *take.*"

"It sounds like nonsense. Why didn't you take?"

"Do you really want to know?"

He nodded.

She sighed. It seemed she'd have to tell him what happened. "Perhaps you are acquainted with Sir Digby Pettleworth."

He nodded again. "He gives dandies a bad name. What did he do to you?"

"He offered for me. Or more precisely, for my dowry. I suppose my refusal wounded his vanity, for he then proceeded to do his utmost to ruin me socially."

"What exactly did he do?"

"He spread it about that I had set my cap at him, but that any man of taste would prefer a debtor's prison to marriage with a lady with so little grace and countenance. Pretty soon I became known as the Homely Hoyden, and my only suitors were those who were on the brink of ruin."

"The ass! I wish I'd been around to teach him a lesson!" The bay tossed his head at the ferocity of Julian's tone.

Harry smiled. She couldn't help feeling flattered that Julian would have championed her so hotly.

"Thank you," she said. "It's good to know you would have come to my rescue, but really, I don't think there's anything you could have done to help."

"I would have thrashed Pettleworth to an inch of his life. Perhaps it's still not too late?"

Again, Harry felt warmed by his eagerness to defend her. Despite herself, she found herself wondering what it would be like to have someone like Julian always willing to protect her. She suppressed the treacherous thought; she didn't need any man's protection. Besides, Julian would have acted in exactly the same manner had she really been his sister.

She shook her head. "There's no need to be so blood-thirsty on my account. I left London soon afterward, and I assure you I am perfectly happy with the life I lead now. None of the men I met in London would have tolerated marriage to an eccentric lady with a passion for breeding and training horses."

"You don't know that," said Julian.

He looked at Harry, trying to see her as the *ton* would have seen her during her debut. Her hair was a soft shade of brown, a warm color like November leaves, although it was pulled back in an unbecoming, severe style. Her eyes were a light blue-gray, and rather fetch-ing when they sparkled with laughter, which happened often enough while they were together. But perhaps Harry hadn't laughed much in London.

He scrutinized her facial features, but decided he couldn't tell if she was pretty or not. She was just Harry, his friend from childhood. He had seen her face too many times; it was so familiar to him that he could not pass a judgment on it. But surely she wasn't homely.

As for her figure—well, she was of average height. No one could call her a Long Meg, nor could any per-son say she was a poor little dab of a creature, either. Neither was she particularly thin nor particularly fat, as far as he could tell. Most ladies had their riding habits tailored closely to show off their figures to the best ad-vantage, but not Harry. All of her clothing was rather loose and shapeless, giving little impression of the fig-ure beneath. She claimed it was comfortable, but Julian suddenly wondered if Harry had deliberately cultivated her dowdiness as a defense against those who would judge her by such superficial standards.

"Harry, not everyone is so shallow," he said. "You were merely unfortunate in some of the people you met. Your Aunt Claudia is a dear, but she wasn't the right person to oversee your come-out, or choose your clothes. Well, she can't see five inches past her nose! Believe me, dressed to the nines, with the right friends to help you, you'd do very well."

"I don't care for having friends who esteem me only for my connections and attire. Even less for a husband who courted me for money alone."

"That's why you should marry me."

"Oh, you *are* stubborn!" She laughed as they turned to make their way back home.

Having taken his luncheon with Harry and her family, Julian remounted his now rested horse and made his way back to town. As he rode, he pondered what Harry had said about her Season. She had spoken lightly, easily disparaging those who had hurt her. But hurt her they had.

As a young, athletic, and wealthy peer, he had never been the target of unkind wit; but now he could see how it could be used against an unsuspecting innocent from the country.

This must be why Harry was so adamant against marriage. Strange, he'd never thought about her marrying anyone. She was just his friend Harry, and would remain so, a fixture at Woodford Park, always to be relied upon, the sister he'd never had. Why hadn't he ever wondered at her not being interested in what the vast majority of young ladies were obsessed with?

Clearly, she was convinced that no man could value her for herself. Julian felt another stab of anger, and an unexpected protectiveness, at the thought of Harry's fragile, youthful confidence being so thoughtlessly destroyed. On the heels of that thought followed a picture of what Harry's life would be like if he married her and did not change his ways.

People would say that they had married for convenience, to join two of the largest estates in Kent, and expect him to pursue his mistresses while ignoring his unfashionable wife. Harry would be subjected to still more cruel gossip.

Well, he wouldn't let that happen. He would marry her, and he'd be the perfect example of the devoted husband. He'd guide her in choosing a new and becoming wardrobe, and convince her to make her reentry into society as the new Viscountess Debenham. He'd enlist the help of all the good-hearted people he knew to make her feel welcome, and he'd teach the fops and nasty cats who had snubbed her what a grave mistake they had made. This time, none would dare belittle Harry, or they'd have Julian to reckon with!

Three

Throughout April and into the beginning of May, Julian continued to successfully avoid the many temptations the Metropolis offered a handsome and wealthy young peer. He decided not to undermine Harry's fragile confidence by relating any details of the lures various ladies used to entice him, but those lures were many and varied.

When the audacious Lady Heatherton invited him to a select dinner party, and he discovered that the company consisted of only himself and his hostess (Lord Heatherton being conveniently out of town), he managed to quickly and carefully extricate himself from the hopeful lady's embrace.

When Miss Fairgood "accidentally" got herself locked into her father's conservatory with him, Julian broke a window to get them out before enough time passed for her eager relations to declare them compromised.

And those were just two of many similar incidents.

Julian was beginning to be a trifle annoyed. Word had somehow gotten round that he was reforming his ways, and all of London seemed outraged at this change in the natural order of things. Men roasted him mercilessly over his reformation, but the ladies were even worse.

Instead of giving him up as a lost cause, they seemed to regard him as a challenge. He found himself the target of more feminine traps and wiles than he had ever encountered since he had come to town. It was as if half the females in London were conspiring to break his resolution.

The devil of it was that Julian adored women. Slender willowy ones, curvy voluptuous ones. They all had such pleasing smiles, such soft voices, and they always smelled of lavender or roses or some other heady fragrance, expressly designed to entice the helpless male of the species. And they seemed to enjoy his attentions so much, he hated to disappoint them.

Still, he'd had no real difficulty resisting any individual lady's advances. There was no particular female, of easy virtue or otherwise, that invaded his dreams. Nevertheless, he found himself feeling restless at night, and unable to fall asleep with his usual ease.

No doubt it was the strain of avoiding so many ambitious females. The only respite he got was on Tuesdays, when he rode out to Kent to visit Harry. At least *she* wasn't pursuing him like a hound after a fox.

When he was with Harry, walking or riding, or playing chess with her in her drawing room, Aunt Claudia nodding peacefully in the corner, he could relax his guard.

What he couldn't figure out was why on Tuesday nights, after riding fifteen miles out from London, spending several hours with Harry, then riding fifteen miles back to London, he *still* couldn't fall asleep.

As the weeks went by, Harry continued to enjoy Julian's weekly visits. He often brought her small gifts, sweets one time, a treatise on horse-breeding the next, but she reminded herself that they meant nothing. He'd brought her gifts in the past, and no doubt he did the same for all his other lady friends.

It was a pleasant time, but now and then Harry felt just a little sadness that it would soon be over. She could see just a hint of strain, an unaccustomed tautness in Julian's demeanor, no doubt due to the effort of renouncing his accustomed pleasures. It was merely a matter of time before he succumbed to some charmer's wiles.

Meanwhile, she would enjoy this bright interlude in her life while she could.

Harry drew her bow, and took careful aim at the target set up on the lawn at Woodford Park. She let the arrow fly, and was pleased to see it hit the target a mere finger's breadth from the bull's-eye.

"Good shot!" said Julian as he took his place in front of the target. His own arrow flew slightly awry, and hit one of the outer rings of the target.

"I think *you* are a trifle out of practice," said Harry with a smile.

Julian returned her smile. "When we are married, you must give me lessons every day."

Harry decided his smile was utterly too engaging, even as she dwelt briefly on the blissful image of married life that his words conjured up. Sternly, she reminded herself that it was an illusion.

"I am afraid you are doomed to disappointment," she said, shooting again. Her second arrow landed close to the first.

Julian's second shot was no better than his first, but Harry's third arrow completed a neat, small triangle around the bull's-eye.

"It's deuced warm out here," Julian complained. He removed his coat and threw it on the garden seat behind them, before taking his place in front of the target again. Harry watched him as he took aim, more slowly this time.

His blond hair and white shirt shone, almost dazzling Harry's eyes in the bright sunshine. As he drew a leg back in the proper stance, the taut musculature of his arms visible through the fabric of his sleeve, she had to admit Julian cut a fine figure. No wonder there were scores of silly females ready to make perfect fools of themselves over his charming smile and broad shoulders. Thank goodness she was not one of them!

Julian shot again, then they went together to the target to retrieve their arrows.

"You've been enjoying my Tuesday visits, haven't you?" asked Julian as they returned to their earlier position.

Harry decided his voice had a suspiciously silky quality. It was not difficult to see where his question led.

"I suppose so," she said in a carefully nonchalant tone. "You are, perhaps, a slightly more lively conversationalist than Aunt Claudia."

Julian choked on a laugh just as he let his first arrow fly. It missed the target entirely.

"Thank you for the compliment, m'dear," he said. "But you must admit it's been fun, and marriage would be even better. Why don't we just end this silly wager and let everyone know we are engaged?"

Harry looked back at Julian. There was a candid, winning light in his eyes. She couldn't help feeling flattered by his eagerness, but it would not do to let him know that.

"We are not engaged," she said, slightly vexed to see her first shot hit the rim of the target.

"We're not engaged . . . *yet*," said Julian, and shot his second arrow. This time his aim was better. "But you can't deny that I've stayed virtuous for almost two months now. All I have to do is endure one more, and I'll be the winner."

She looked away, unsettled by his confidence but unwilling to let him see it.

"More likely you're afraid your resolution is about to crack, and you are trying to get round me with your cajolery. It won't work," she said, shooting again. Her second shot was no better than the first.

"Very well, but you can't fault me for trying," said Julian. He shot again, and Harry saw his third arrow strike the target less than an inch from the bull's-eye.

She caught him watching her as she prepared for her third shot, still with that roguish smile on his lips. She felt an errant blush creep into her cheeks. She couldn't help it; the way Julian acted, it was dangerously easy to think he really wanted her. Of course, a rake would have to have just such winning ways in order to be so successful.

She let the arrow fly, but this time she was unsurprised to see it go far wide of the mark. Clearly, her wager with Julian was playing havoc with her composure.

"Have you had enough?" asked Julian, grinning.

She nodded, suppressing the foolish, competitive urge to continue. In her current state of mind she wouldn't be able to shoot straight, and Julian would tease her mercilessly.

"Let us just walk a little, then. I have a favor to ask you," said Julian.

"What is it?" she asked. The wheedling tone in his voice aroused her suspicion; she wondered if his earlier request had been made only to soften her in preparation for what he really wanted to ask her.

"Can I tell my uncles that I've offered for you?"

Of course, she thought, with an unexpected, foolish little pang. She had almost forgotten that his uncles were the reason behind his proposal and their bet. She had almost forgotten that she was not the sort of female to inspire any gentleman with such ardent impatience to marry her.

"No," she replied, hoping her voice didn't betray her irrational disappointment. "It's against the rules we agreed upon."

"We could agree to change the rules."

"Why would I want to do that?" she said, lifting her chin a little.

"If I tell my uncles I've offered for you, I think they might be persuaded to allow me a hand in managing the estate."

The thought of Julian's uncles and his estate steadied her. "I see that that could be a good thing," she replied. "But won't they be disappointed when we don't marry?"

He let out an exasperated sigh. "We *will* marry. In any case, I don't intend to lie to them. I'll just tell them I plan to marry you, which is nothing more than the truth. I know it's not enough to convince them to end the trust, but for now all I want is to be allowed to make some changes in how things are being run."

Harry struggled to resist the appeal in his eyes. Julian was acting impetuously, and if she didn't stop him, it would hurt them both.

"I don't see why you must be in such a great hurry," she protested.

"There are so many things that need doing here. I may not know as much as I should about farming, but even I can tell we're years behind. There are some improvements I'd like to make *this* season, not next. And some of the laborers' cottages are desperately in need of repair. I don't want them to have to wait any longer. Please, Harry, will you help me?"

Harry looked down, troubled. What Julian said was true. The Ardleigh estate could not be said to be run-down, but still it would benefit from more vigorous and farsighted management. Harry knew that beneath his gaiety, Julian cared for his land, and for the tenants and laborers who worked it. In time he'd make a splendid landlord. It was a crying shame that his uncles didn't recognize that fact, and that they were practically forcing him into an impetuous marriage in order to earn their approval.

Then it occurred to her that she might be able to help Julian without actually committing to marry him. As he'd suggested, he could just tell his uncles he'd offered for her. They would never suspect she'd refused him. Perhaps it was the tiniest bit deceitful to let them think that, but it would be worth it, for Julian's sake.

After a decent interval, she could cry off from the pretended arrangement. Hopefully by that time, Julian's uncles would be convinced of his competence to take over the estate. Julian would get what he wanted, and have something more meaningful to do with his life than merely racketing about London. He wouldn't have to rush into a doomed marriage with her or anyone else, before he was truly ready to settle down.

Of course, he wouldn't *want* to marry her then.

Firmly, Harry told herself that it would be a great relief not to have him plaguing her to do so anymore.

She took a deep breath. "Very well," she said. "You can tell your uncles you have offered for me, but you must swear them to secrecy. If they ask, tell them you know I would hate all the fuss and attention an engagement would bring. I'm known to be a recluse, so they shouldn't be surprised."

Smiling, Julian hooked an arm around her waist, and swung her around in a broad circle. "Thank you! I knew you would help me."

"Set me down!" she insisted, and after one more circle, he did so.

Harry felt quite breathless and dizzy, no doubt from the spinning. She looked around. Fortunately, there was no one about.

"What if someone had seen us?" she scolded, when she had caught her breath.

"They would realize we are a courting couple," he replied.

She looked away, to hide the blush that had sprung back into her cheeks, and reminded herself of the motives behind Julian's behavior.

He didn't desire her, despite his apparent eagerness. For the first time, Harry found herself shaken by a real fear that he might win the wager. At the same time, a tiny voice inside her suggested she wished it, too. If Julian proved faithful for three months, didn't that mean something?

The internal voice of reason intervened, reminding Harry that she didn't love Julian, and that a few months of happiness—for surely that would be as long as it would last—were nothing when compared to a lifetime of regret for both of them. She had to prevent that at all costs, but now that she had agreed to delude his uncles, was she encouraging Julian to think he might succeed?

"I hope I'm doing the right thing," she murmured, half to herself.

"Of course you are," Julian answered in a comforting voice. "What could possibly go wrong?"

As Julian predicted, his uncles were delighted when he invited them to his London house to notify them of his intention to marry Harriet.

In their eyes, she was the most suitable of brides. Certainly, her passion for horses and preference for country life made her a bit of an Eccentric, but her reputation was spotless, the Woodford name an old and respected one, and her prospective inheritance large enough to be a welcome addition to the already considerable Ardleigh fortune.

Impressed with their nephew's good judgment, they readily agreed to send letters to the Ardleigh steward directing him to begin taking his orders from young Lord Debenham. They also promised Julian that on his wedding day, they would commence the legal procedures required to formally end the trust.

With some reluctance, they acquiesced to Julian's request to keep the matter quiet. It was a bit odd of the young lady to prefer a secret engagement, but it was no great matter, after all.

Of course, they reasoned, Julian couldn't possibly have meant them to keep such good news from their own wives. . . .

Four

A few days later, Julian found Harry in the Woodford stables, changing a poultice. Julian recognized the injured horse as an elderly hack that Harry still rode occasionally. It was like her to attend to the loyal old beast herself, rather than leaving the task to a groom.

He waited patiently as she finished fastening the bandage, patted the afflicted horse, and straightened up. Then he cleared his voice before announcing his presence.

"Hello, Harry."

She turned, and a delighted smile lit up her face.

"Julian! What brings you here today?" she asked as she came out of the stall into the stable yard.

Julian decided she looked rather fetching, even with a wisp of straw caught in the thick coil of hair atop her head. On impulse, he reached a hand up and brushed it away.

"I have something to tell you," he said, and regretted seeing her smile fade. Did he see the hint of a blush in her face?

"What is it?" she asked, moving away from him and beginning to walk toward the house. "Have you come to tell me I've won our little wager?"

Was it his imagination, or did her voice sound a trifle

brittle? This was turning out to be even more difficult than he had expected.

"No, not exactly," he replied. "Let's take a turn about the garden, so we can speak privately."

They reached the garden in silence, and began to stroll between beds full of irises, larkspur and early roses. He looked over at Harry. Her cheeks still seemed slightly flushed. She looked uncharacteristically nervous, and yet appealing at the same time. She walked briskly, yet she moved with her usual athletic grace.

He could see she was ill at ease with the prospect of marriage with him, and longed to reassure her. She'd clearly never even been kissed. Lately, he'd found himself thinking how much he'd enjoy teaching her such pleasures, and tried to picture what charms she hid beneath those curst dowdy gowns of hers. However, her matter-of-fact manner had discouraged him from making any advances.

Now he feared he might never get the chance.

"So, what is it?" Harry asked, interrupting his train of thought.

He cleared his throat before replying. "I told my uncles I'd offered for you."

"And?"

"They were delighted, and they agreed to allow me a hand in running the estate."

"I am happy to hear that. But that isn't what you came to tell me, is it?" she asked, looking sharply at him. "You told them you offered for me, and they told someone else. Is that it?"

He nodded, unsure whether to be glad or sorry of her perspicacity. He looked at her face, but it was strangely expressionless.

"Well then, you've broken the rules, so I win."

"No," he argued. "You agreed to change the rules so I could tell my uncles. It's not my fault they told my aunts, who told everybody else."

"But the fact remains that the wager is no longer valid, now that everyone thinks you're engaged to marry me. You'll have to deny the engagement."

"How can I do that? I'd look a damned fool to my uncles, and then it'll be five more years before they let me do *anything.*"

"I shall cry off, then."

Damn! Somehow it hurt to hear how eager Harry was to end the wager. More than ever, Julian was convinced they'd make a perfect match. The trouble was, how could he convince her?

"I've a better idea," he said. "You have to admit, I was winning the wager, so you can't say I'm a rake anymore. You can't deny you've enjoyed our times together, so you can't say we don't suit. Why don't we just send notice of our engagement to the papers and be done with it?"

Harry was silent, and again her expression was hard to read. She had never been so reserved with him before; the strange sense of hurt he'd been feeling increased.

"Why don't you say something?" he coaxed. "Do you really think it would be so awful to be married to me?"

"No, of course not," she said, beginning to climb the steps into the house.

Her tone this time was warmer, more encouraging. Or perhaps she was just trying to spare his feelings.

"So you'll marry me?"

"I didn't say that," she replied swiftly.

"Will you at least allow me the chance to win our wager?"

She glanced at him briefly, then looked away.

"Very well," she said. "There is still a month left, after all."

With that, he had to be content.

That afternoon, after Julian left, Harry went for a long ride. It had been a struggle to maintain a cheerful facade so that neither he, Papa, nor Aunt Claudia would guess at the jumbled state of her emotions.

She should have insisted that they cancel the wager, but Julian had looked so hurt that she'd given in to his pleading. She was clearly a fool; it was really beginning to look as if Julian would win.

She'd be an even greater fool if she flattered herself that Julian was persevering for her sake. Although he was clearly convinced that marriage would benefit them both, she had to remember that all he really wanted was control of the Ardleigh estate.

Why hadn't she remembered that Julian could show great resolution when something he really wanted was at stake? In fact, she didn't doubt now that he could remain faithful to a wife that he loved. He'd make some fortunate lady a wonderful husband one day. Why did the thought make her feel just a trifle forlorn?

Shaking her head, she rode on.

More than ever, Harry was certain that friendship alone would not ensure a happy marriage. Thinking over the past weeks, she realized it would be easy enough to develop a *tendre* for Julian, if she allowed herself to do so. However, that would only make matters worse, for it was impossible to imagine him returning her feelings.

She couldn't allow this to happen. If the worst came

to the worst, she would have to ask Julian to release
her from their agreement. There was no way he could
force her to uphold her side of the bargain, after all.
However, he would think it dishonorable of her to back
out at the last minute. He would be disappointed, even
angry. Even if he eventually forgave her, their friendship
would never be the same.

Harry felt tears prick her eyelids at the thought.

Gloomily, she decided that it would be best if some
lady who didn't care about the rumors of his engagement, perhaps one seeking a casual liaison, lured Julian
into losing the wager. But at this late date, could she
count on such a thing happening?

That week, Julian was annoyed to find that despite
the word of his engagement, the betting-books at several
gaming establishments now recorded wagers on how
long his resolution would hold.

Not only did he have to deal with the widowed count-
ess who stole into his carriage prior to his leaving the
theatre, and others like her, he now had to deal with
various members of the feminine sex who had been
hired by those wishing to profit by his moral downfall.

By now, however, he was grimly determined to succeed. He knew she would never admit it, but he suspected Harry would be hurt if he was unfaithful, now
that all of society thought them engaged. He wouldn't
hurt her for anything; thus, every time temptation beckoned, he thought of her and the estate, and the new life
he planned. He found it was not so very difficult to
resist.

Even when several enterprising young bucks smug-
gled a lovely ladybird in a state of full undress into

Julian's bedchamber, he managed to give the woman her marching orders with very little regret.

Still, sometimes he felt he would explode with longing for all the pleasures he'd had to forego.

The following week, Julian visited Harry as usual; he also spent a few additional days in Kent, becoming more familiar with the details of his estate, and started several projects for its improvement. Harry enjoyed his visit more than ever, but her pleasure in his company was tinged with a sadness at the knowledge that this lovely period in her life would soon be over.

Julian was so eager, and so full of plans, that she couldn't bring herself to ask him to cancel their wager. Afterward, she berated herself for her weakness. Now more than ever, she hoped that something would happen to keep her from having to end things in such a way.

She didn't know what was wrong with all the ladies in London, but it seemed that this Season they weren't pursuing Julian with anything like their usual enthusiasm. After another week of worry and indecision, Harry decided it was time to take matters into her own hands.

Lady Dearing and Troubadour certainly made a lovely picture together, Harry thought as she watched the widow take the dappled gray gelding through his paces. Lady Dearing, in her snug-fitting sapphire blue habit and matching hat, would have been striking on any mount, but she and Troubadour were sure to create quite a sensation the next time she rode in Hyde Park.

Harry suppressed an unexpected pang of envy at the sight. She truly was glad to see Troubadour go to such a kind mistress, and she reminded herself that she wouldn't care for the fashionable life Lady Dearing led. One couldn't go for a brisk gallop in Hyde Park.

"What a delightful creature he is!" exclaimed Lady Dearing as she rode back toward the paddock gate where Harry awaited her. "I will take him, at the price we discussed last time."

"I am delighted you are pleased with him," said Harry.

"No, the pleasure is mine. I do so like dealing with you, Miss Woodford. Men invariably behave condescendingly when a female wishes to choose her own horses; they always think they know better what will suit her than she does!"

Harry smiled, glad of Lady Dearing's willingness to behave unconventionally. It boded well for her own plans.

After Lady Dearing had dismounted and handed the reins to a groom waiting nearby to take Troubadour back to the stables, Harry invited her inside for refreshments. After they settled themselves in the drawing room, and a maidservant brought some tea and cakes, Harry gathered her courage to make her request.

"Miss Woodford, is there something amiss?"

"No, not at all," said Harry, realizing she had been fidgeting with her cup. Her cheeks flushed at the thought of what she was about to ask. "It is merely that I wish to ask a favor of you. You might think it rather odd."

"What is it? You have me all agog with curiosity!"

"Would you please—could you—I would be very grateful if you could induce Lord Debenham to kiss you."

There. The words were said. No doubt Lady Dearing

thought her a lunatic, Harry surmised, even as she tried to gauge the attractive widow's expression.

"You would like me to do *what?*" Lady Dearing's low, musical voice rose to a high note as she looked quizzically at Harry.

Harry's confidence wavered as she repeated her request. "I w-would like you to meet with Lord Debenham, and—and entice him into kissing you."

"But, my dear Miss Woodford! I was under the impression that the two of you were betrothed. Was I wrong?"

"No—well, yes. I think I must explain."

"Please do," said Lady Dearing, an amused smile playing about her lips.

Harry noted the smile with a measure of relief. She'd already decided she would have to trust Lady Dearing with the whole story, and she was glad to see that the woman didn't appear to think that Harry had completely lost her senses. So she told her the entire history of Julian's proposal and their wager, ending with a reiteration of her request for Lady Dearing to use her charms to Julian's undoing.

"But, Miss Woodford—oh, why are we being so formal? You must call me Olivia, and you are Harriet, are you not?"

"Harry, please."

"Harry," repeated Lady Dearing, her voice like a sisterly caress. "Do you truly wish to end your engagement to Debenham? He is such a delightful young man, don't you think?"

"Of course, but we have been friends for so many years, we are practically sister and brother. How could such a marriage succeed?"

"Merely by your learning to regard each other as

something quite different," Lady Dearing replied with a little trill of a laugh.

"I don't wish to offend you, La—Olivia, but I cannot think it so simple. Julian and I lead such different lives. He loves London society, I prefer to stay here. Besides, I am not the sort of female men truly wish to marry."

"How do you know that?"

Harry felt Lady Dearing's brilliant blue-green eyes upon her. She might have been offended at the close scrutiny had she not noticed the kind interest in Lady Dearing's expression, and the gentleness in her voice.

"One Season in London was enough to convince me," she said, hoping Lady Dearing would take the hint and not question her any further. "In any case, I am perfectly content with my life the way it is, and I'm certain that marriage with Julian would be a disaster for both of us. All he's thinking about is gaining control of his estate. He doesn't realize that one day he may fall in love with someone, and *really* wish to marry her. I don't want to stand in his way when that happens."

Harry bit her lip, and looked away in embarrassment. She felt as if she was about to cry, but that was foolish. She was doing what was best for both her and Julian, so there was absolutely no reason to be dismal about it.

"Well, why don't you just tell him so? He cannot force you to marry him, and I'm sure he wouldn't do it, if he knew the strength of your feelings against the match."

"I may be obliged to do that, but Julian would be so angry! He will say I broke faith with him. It would be so much better if he just lost the wager. Then, he might realize he's not ready to marry yet. He might not rush out to find someone else."

"You may be right. It seems as if it would be a good thing if he were to lose the wager," said Lady Dearing, thoughtfully. After a pause, she added, "But why are you asking *me* to lead him into temptation?"

Lady Dearing's expression was difficult to read. Harry worried suddenly that her friend had taken offense at the suggestion. Lady Dearing always seemed so cheerful about her reputation as a merry widow, but it was possible that her carefree attitude hid an unexpected sensitivity.

"Well, it seems that none of the ladies in London have tried very hard to engage Julian's attention," Harry replied cautiously. She saw a twinkle in Lady Dearing's eye; relieved, she continued. "You are so very beautiful, and lively. I am sure you could tempt Julian, if only you tried."

Harry sat silently watching as Lady Dearing stared absently out the window for a few moments. Finally, the widow turned her gaze back at Harry, with a decisive expression on her face.

"Well, my dear Harry, I've thought about it, and I have decided to help you."

"Oh, thank you so much!" Impulsively, Harry got up from her chair. She was about to embrace Lady Dearing when the widow held up a hand in a halting gesture.

"But I cannot do exactly what you have requested. You see, I have a—how should I explain it? Oh, you are no missish little girl! I can tell you. I already have a gentleman friend, a lover if you will. Unfortunately, he is of a rather jealous nature—so it is out of the question at present for me to try to flirt with your Julian. Contrary to what you might have heard, I am *not* the sort of woman who finds it amusing to have men fight over her. You would not wish your friend to be hurt over me, would you?"

"No, of course not," said Harry, despondent. What other sort of help could Lady Dearing possibly have to give her? "Do you know of some other lady who can do this?" she asked.

"Yes, I do." A triumphant little smile played about Lady Dearing's lips.

"Who is it?" Harry asked eagerly.

"You, dear."

Five

Harry flinched as Lady Dearing's maid inserted another pin into her hair, and wondered for perhaps the hundredth time why she had ever allowed Lady Dearing to persuade her into this masquerade. At the time, it had seemed her only option, but it was clearly hopeless. She was a dowd, and an Antidote, and no disguise could transform her into the sort of female that would attract Julian's notice.

"Stop twitching, dear. We are almost done," said Lady Dearing.

Harry forced herself to sit still, wondering what she would see when Lady Dearing allowed her to look at herself in the mirror. She didn't know why the widow seemed so amused, or why she was so determined that Harry not see herself until every finishing detail was in place. All Harry could feel was trepidation. However, there was nothing to do now but to forge ahead with their plan.

"There. What do you think, my lady?" asked Lady Dearing's maid.

"It is perfect. Dear Harry, come and see how attractive you look!"

Obediently, she got up and walked over to the oval

cheval glass in the corner of Lady Dearing's dressing room.

And froze.

She was indeed transformed. She knew her hair had been dyed, but she hadn't suspected how different her face would look framed in raven-black locks, which were braided and looped in an elaborate classical style, with a slender silver cord threaded through. Lady Dearing herself had applied a subtle layer of powder and rouge over her face, and darkened her lips with a bright red salve.

Even without a mask, Harry could barely recognize herself. Perhaps there was a chance Julian would not recognize her. But would he find her at all appealing?

Then she looked at her dress, and gasped.

"Oh dear!" she exclaimed. "Your dressmaker made it too short. My ankles are in full view!"

Lady Dearing only chuckled. "And very pretty ankles they are, too. Now, Harry, this is no time to be a prude."

"I'm not a prude, but I have no desire to look foolish!" she retorted, noting with shock the way the filmy white silk draped about her figure, leaving one shoulder and breast practically bare.

"Nonsense! You are lovely. What a crime to have hidden such a figure away all these years! I am truly envious. Here, put on the sandals."

Harry sat down, and allowed Lady Dearing's maid to lace a pair of silver sandals around her feet. The sandals were just as scandalous as the rest of her apparel.

"Don't look so frightened, you goose!" said Lady Dearing in a heartening tone. "You could break hearts tonight, if you wish. Wait, you need a little scent."

Harry sneezed and rebelled at the heady perfume Lady Dearing offered. After a few minutes of discussion they compromised on a lighter floral scent, which Harry dabbed onto her wrists and throat as Lady Dearing directed.

"Very well, then," said Lady Dearing. "Here are your mask and domino, and don't forget the arrows and quiver. Of course, you must wear the domino open for the best effect. And remember to keep your mask on!"

Harry put on the shimmering white cloak, and took the half mask from Lady Dearing. She put it on, and observed the effect in the mirror. It was a lovely, silvery thing, adorned with a crescent moon that arched exotically over her forehead. She slung the little quiver of paper arrows over one shoulder, and the toy silver bow over the other, and stifled a nervous giggle. The goddess Diana!

"So what do you think now?" asked Lady Dearing.

"I'm confused," said Harry. "I thought the goddess Diana was determined to remain chaste."

"Men always desire what is forbidden," replied Lady Dearing. "They like a challenge. Venus would have been too obvious."

"Perhaps you are right. And Diana is a huntress, so that fits in with our scheme," said Harry nervously, still staring at her reflection. "Are you certain I don't look ridiculous?"

"Of course you look ridiculous, dear. Everyone does at a true costume ball. But you look enchanting as well."

"Enchanting?" Such a word had never been used to describe *her*.

"Trust me, my dear. Your friend Julian doesn't stand a chance."

Harry tried to keep Lady Dearing's encouraging words in mind as the widow's carriage swept her toward the house in Richmond where the masquerade ball was to be held. Nervously, she reviewed her plan.

She would enter by a side door Lady Dearing had told her of, which led almost directly to the ballroom. There she would dance and flirt as Lady Dearing had taught her, but give her name to no one and speak in a huskier voice than usual. She would find Julian, then lure him into the garden and induce him to kiss her, using one ruse or another. Lady Dearing had given her a number of suggestions.

The deed done, Harry would leave before matters progressed any further; Lady Dearing's discreet servants would drive her back to Kent, where she'd spend the remainder of the night at the secluded cottage of her old Nurse. She would wash the dye out of her hair and walk back home. Everyone would think she'd spent the entire time with Nurse, who had obligingly agreed to pretend she was ailing. Then, if all went well, Julian would arrive to tell her she had won. If only she could be sure nothing would go wrong!

Julian was sure to attend the masquerade; the hostess, Mrs. Gorewell, was his cousin. In her youth, Mrs. Gorewell had disgraced herself by running away with a clerk, and had not been accepted back into society since making such a misalliance. Her husband had prospered, inheriting a business from his wealthy employer, and since then the couple had taken to lavish entertaining. Their rather daring parties were attended by a piquant mix of guests: persons in Trade, actors, artists, and members of the *haut ton* who were not so high in the instep as to cut Mrs. Gorewell's acquaintance. This last category included Julian.

Still, Harry couldn't be at all certain she would be able to attract him. Despite her altered appearance, she still found it difficult to see herself as a *femme fatale*. And was it right to deceive him so? Even if it was for his own good? And what if he recognized her? That would put the fat in the fire indeed!

She continued to worry until the coach slowed; the unpleasant flutter in the pit of her stomach increased as she realized she had reached her destination. A few minutes later, she had succeeded in entering the house without attracting any undue notice. Despite a shaky feeling in her legs, she swiftly made her way toward the ballroom. Once there, however, she stopped short on the threshold.

Julian had once told Harry that his cousin spared no effort to make her parties memorable. He hadn't exaggerated. Mrs. Gorewell must have hired a veritable army of carpenters, painters, and seamstresses to transform the ballroom into an appropriately brilliant setting for a masquerade. Immediately to her right, Harry saw colorful pennants hanging over the turrets of a makeshift castle; in the corner to her left, sand, potted palms, and exotic draperies suggested an eastern desert. In the far left corner rose the quaint roofs of several miniature Chinese pagodas, while in the far right corner, a row of Ionic columns under a sweep of blue fabric painted with white clouds could only be Mount Olympus.

Against this colorful backdrop, musicians played, and Mrs. Gorewell's guests, arrayed variously as knights and princesses, satyrs and nymphs, gods and goddesses, either danced or stood about chatting in small groups.

A magical setting, where magical things could happen.

Harry looked about, but she couldn't see Julian. Perhaps he hadn't arrived yet, or was in one of the adjacent rooms. She was so busy looking that it took her several moments to realize that most of the guests who were not dancing, and even some of those who were, had their eyes on her.

Oh dear! Despite Lady Dearing's efforts, she must still look ridiculous, else why would they all stare so? For an instant, Harry wrestled with the urge to take immediate flight.

Then a young gentleman dressed as Robin Hood approached her and stammered out a request for the next dance. She accepted, realizing it would be cowardly to run away without having made some attempt to execute her plan.

As she danced, she found herself relaxing slightly. Far from laughing at her, young Robin Hood was inclined to stammer when he spoke, and redden when she smiled at him. He must be very shy, she thought; perhaps that was why he'd taken pity on her earlier embarrassment, and why he was paying her some hesitant compliments. She dreaded the end of the dance, for she didn't dare hope that there would be others at the ball who would show the same kindness.

By some miracle, her hand was immediately claimed for the next dance by a nautical gentleman attired as Neptune, wearing a blue robe and carrying a trident. Surprisingly, he paid her several broad compliments as well, even though he seemed more worldly than Robin Hood, and not at all shy.

When the second dance ended, she still hadn't spotted Julian; but to her surprise, she found herself surrounded by aspiring partners and besieged with offers of refreshment. Perhaps she did look rather attractive after all, she thought, recklessly downing a glass of champagne. She peered between her admirers, hoping to catch a glimpse of Julian. What would she do if he didn't come?

Her eyes were still roving when she heard one of her companions curse under his breath. She saw another gentleman seeking entry into the circle around her, and her newfound confidence shattered as she saw who it was. Sir Digby Pettleworth!

It was easy enough to recognize him; apparently he disdained wearing a true costume. His simple mask did not hide his handsome but supercilious features. Harry's heart sank as she watched him raise a quizzing-glass to observe her more closely.

To hide her foreboding, she turned and laughed at something Neptune had just said to her, even as a host of anxious questions assailed her. What if Sir Digby recognized her? But no, that was foolish; of course he wouldn't remember her after so many years. But what if he once again decided to pronounce her unworthy of his interest? Would her new admirers desert her? If they did, how would she ever regain her courage enough to try to attract Julian?

As she fretted, Sir Digby seemed to complete his assessment.

"O bright and glorious goddess Diana, take pity on a lowly worshipper. Please grant me just one dance," said Sir Digby, in the oily voice she remembered so well.

She couldn't help staring at him for a moment. She had never expected this! She could hear admiration, but also a strange hint of desperation in his voice. Taking a second look, Harry realized that the past five years had not treated Sir Digby kindly. His face seemed yellow and lined from dissipation, and he was developing a paunch. She felt an unexpected stirring of pity for him. Still, the thought of dancing with him filled her with revulsion.

She was on the verge of telling him that she was already engaged for all of the remaining dances, when she and the gentlemen around her all started at the sound of a high-pitched shriek coming from somewhere behind them.

"Oh, Digby! Dear Sir Dig-bee!" the voice squealed.

Harry turned to see a stout Shepherdess beckoning toward Sir Digby from the entrance to the ballroom. The lady was a rather frightening sight, with her brassy yellow hair and an ominous-looking crook in her hand. Her expression was menacing.

"I am desolated, but I must leave you. Perhaps later?" said Sir Digby.

She gave a little shake of her head. Looking crestfallen, he bowed and quickly made his way toward the Shepherdess.

"Poor Pettleworth," said Neptune, watching him leave.

A portly gentleman, appropriately costumed as Henry VIII, nodded and asked, "Quite rolled-up this time, ain't he?"

"He must be, to pursue Miss Dudley," said a third gentleman.

"Oh, is she wealthy?" Harry asked, unable to restrain her curiosity.

"Her father is a banker who wishes her to marry into society," said Neptune. "But with the exception of Sir Digby, no one seems to be quite desperate enough to pay court to her."

"*I* wouldn't, not if it was the choice between her and a debtor's prison!" said Henry VIII, with a booming, rather unpleasant laugh.

"Oh, poor girl," said Harry.

"She's known to be quite a shrew. It'll be poor Sir Digby soon enough," said Neptune.

Seeing the proprietary way Miss Dudley looked at Sir Digby, Harry couldn't help but feel that this prediction was correct. It seemed a fitting end for him, and yet she found she couldn't help pitying him a little. He was pathetic, and she should never have allowed his petty cruelty to drive her into a five-year seclusion. Perhaps, if she had shown more courage, she might have eventually found her place in society. Perhaps . . .

But this was no time for idle musings on what might have been! She had to look for Julian. She scanned the ballroom, but still couldn't see him, so she agreed to dance with Henry VIII. She found the stout gentleman moderately unpleasant, but she'd danced with most of the others already, and didn't want to encourage them too much.

She continued to scan through the crowd, even as she danced. She was so absorbed in searching for Julian, she hardly noticed the way Henry VIII gave her hand a tight squeeze every time the movement of the dance gave him an opportunity to touch her. Harry merely looked coldly at him whenever he did so.

Finally she spotted Julian, standing near the entrance. He looked magnificent, in a red tunic over a coat of chain mail, a sword at his side and a shield slung over his shoulder. A light helmet covered his head and the upper half of his face, but his smile was unmistakable. He turned slightly to speak to someone, and she saw that the shield was white as snow, with a red cross emblazoned in the center.

Sir Galahad the Pure!

She almost giggled. Then she reminded herself that this was no laughing matter. No doubt Julian had chosen to play the virtuous, celibate knight as a deliberate if humorous message to warn off ambitious females.

Then she caught him looking back at her, and something about his stance made her think perhaps she'd captured his interest. She met his gaze, then looked away, as Lady Dearing had told her to do. The next time the movement of the dance had her facing in his direction, she gave him another coy, fleeting smile. Unfortunately, her partner was facing her and took the gesture for himself.

"Ah, you are not made of ice after all, divine Diana!" he said thickly as he came forward to twirl her around and lead her into the next movement.

As she heard the music come to an end, she sighed with relief. However, instead of releasing her, Henry VIII grasped her hand tightly, and began to walk her toward the open doors at one end of the ballroom. She realized then that there was a strong aroma of spirits about him. He was also much stronger than she had expected, despite his protruding stomach. She wondered what to do. Lady Dearing's instructions hadn't included how to deal with amorous drunkards.

She protested and tried to pull away, but he went on, impervious. She looked about, but no one seemed to be paying any attention to them. Her throat tightened with panic, and she wondered if she would be able to scream if she had to. She recoiled at the thought of making such a scene, yet it might be necessary.

"Unhand the lady!" she heard from behind her. Thank God, it was Julian's voice!

"Why should I? The tart's mine!" grunted Henry VIII.

"Because I'll pitch you headfirst into the rosebushes if you don't let her go. In fact, you had better leave. I know my cousin and her husband do not tolerate such boorish behavior at their parties."

Henry VIII looked up at Julian's unsmiling face. For a moment, Harry feared there would be a fight; then Henry VIII apparently decided his odds were not good against an irate, athletic, and apparently sober young gentleman. He released Harry, mumbled an apology, and wandered off aimlessly.

Harry leaned against a pillar in relief.

"He didn't hurt you, did he?" Julian asked gently.

"No, J—" Harry stopped in confusion, realizing she'd almost called him by name. Now that she was safe, she had to gather her wits and try to execute her plan. Remembering to disguise her voice, she continued, "Just frightened me a little. I'm afraid I am unaccustomed to such behavior."

"No lady should ever be accustomed to such behavior."

"Thank you so much for rescuing me. Sir Galahad, is it not?" she said with what she hoped was an inviting smile.

"Entirely at your service, Goddess Diana," said Julian, with a graceful bow. "Rescuing damsels in distress is my specialty."

Harry relaxed slightly. She thought she saw an admiring glint in his eyes, even through the mask, and was encouraged to see he was disposed to flirt. Hopefully, she could follow his lead.

"And what reward do you expect for your brave deed?" she asked, with another arch smile.

"A gallant knight knows that a brave deed is its own reward," he replied.

Momentarily, Harry panicked. It seemed Julian really was able to resist temptation. But she couldn't give up so easily. "Oh, but such selfless gallantry deserves some reward," she replied. "At least one dance, perhaps?"

She thought he stiffened slightly, and could almost see him trying to decide whether to accept her bold offer.

Then he smiled, and said, "How could I spurn such a glorious reward?" He took her hand, and led her back into the ballroom.

Just then the musicians began to play a waltz.

Harry stiffened as Julian took her hand in his, and put his other hand around her waist. Then she forced herself to relax. The waltz had not yet become fashionable when she had made her debut into society, but luckily Lady Dearing had had the forethought to teach her the steps. Harry knew that Julian's hand on her waist was merely a part of the dance and not necessarily amorous. Still, his touch felt amazingly, disturbingly intimate.

He smiled down at her in an encouraging manner; no doubt he thought she was still unsettled by her earlier encounter with Henry VIII. Nervously, she smiled back. As the music began, she tried to relax and follow his lead.

Suddenly she realized that despite all the years they'd known each other, it was the first time they'd danced together. She wasn't surprised to find Julian was a graceful dancer. After some initial stiffness, she found herself responding easily to his guidance and even enjoying the gliding and twirling movements of the dance. She remembered now that she had always enjoyed dancing; it was just the accompanying flirtation and small talk that she had found difficult.

Pray heaven she could find it in herself to flirt now.

She looked up at Julian, and saw him looking down at her.

"I was wondering when you would look up, fair Diana," he said.

"I am sorry, Sir Knight," she replied. "I was merely minding my steps. I have only waltzed once before." She blushed as soon as the words left her mouth. It hadn't been her intention to appear so unsophisticated.

"Oh, but you dance *divinely!*"

She chuckled. "As a goddess should?"

He laughed, too. She watched his face, but found it difficult to read, particularly since his eyes were partially hidden by the helmet. He was flirting lightly, elegantly, and very likely it meant nothing. She would have to step up the pace of her efforts, or it would all be in vain.

She forced her lips into a worldly pout, and asked, "So, Sir Galahad, do you make a habit of rescuing damsels in distress?"

"I do. Of course, damsels in distress are always extremely beautiful, so it is no great hardship to do so."

Oh, he did have a smooth tongue! But perhaps it was all just in play. Had she really captured his interest?

"Now, is it true what they say, that you are never tempted by the ladies you rescue?" she asked. She had hoped to sound coy, but even to her own ears her voice sounded breathless.

"If there were no temptation, there would be no virtue," he said. "In fact, the greater the temptation, the greater the virtue."

Perhaps it was the champagne, but Harry was beginning to enjoy this game of double meanings.

"So how virtuous are you feeling tonight?" she asked recklessly.

He paused, and she noticed that his breathing had quickened.

"Very," he replied briefly.

Heavens, he *was* tempted! Harry felt herself being swept up in a whirlwind of emotions: excitement, elation, and a slight, odd tinge of disappointment. That was foolish; she would lose the bet if he remained faithful to her. She couldn't let him win. That was why she was here.

Julian must have sensed her agitation.

"Are you feeling quite well?" he asked.

"I do feel a trifle warm," she replied, recognizing her opportunity. "Please, Sir Galahad, may I trouble you for one more favor? Will you escort me for a turn in the gardens? I'm sure some fresh air will set me to rights, but I fear going alone."

He hesitated, hopefully because he was fighting temptation. She was clearly demented, for she couldn't decide whether to be thrilled, disappointed, or terrified when he finally nodded.

"Very well, fair Goddess. Your wish is my command."

Six

Julian led the mysterious lady out of the crowd. He didn't think anyone noticed as they passed through the open doors at the end of the ballroom, into the relative coolness of the June night.

He probably shouldn't be heading into the gardens with her, but what could he do? Leave her to be prey to more ravening oafs like that Henry VIII? He couldn't do it.

Despite her exotic beauty and her ready wit, the lady had an odd air of vulnerability. Poor little soul, she'd had a nasty fright. He couldn't help pitying her, even if catty persons would say she had brought it on herself by wearing such a deliciously scandalous costume. Somehow, he had the feeling that this masquerade was the first time she'd done anything like this.

He also had the strangest feeling that he'd met her before, but that was impossible. He would have remembered, surely. That slender figure so tantalizingly revealed through the classical drapery she wore. Those adorable little feet, in those delightfully frivolous sandals. The graceful line of her neck, those soft, white shoulders. Her scent—sweet and innocently alluring—lilies of the valley, he realized. No, he couldn't have forgotten this exquisite lady.

Wordlessly, he led her toward a stone seat in a secluded corner of the garden, under a fragrant, overgrown rose arbor. Nearby a fountain gurgled, the sounds of music faint in the distance. Julian could hear other couples moving about in other corners of the garden, but he and the mysterious lady seemed quite alone. She sat down, and he joined her, keeping a discreet distance between them. He reminded himself that he was here merely to protect her, while she took time to recover her composure.

Silently, he watched her. He really ought to look away, but found that he couldn't. He noted the quickness of her breath and the fast beating of the pulse in the hollow of her throat, and found himself longing to press his lips just there.

He looked away then, and just in time. What was wrong with him? He'd exercised perfect self-control for so long; he was just two weeks from victory. So why was he struggling tonight to keep from gathering a lovely stranger into his arms?

He cleared his throat, and asked, "Are you feeling better now?"

She nodded. "I am quite well, thank you. But there is something I must tell you . . ." She went silent, twisting her hands nervously in her lap.

"What is it?" he asked, curiosity aroused.

"I have lied to you," she said. "I am *not* unwell. I asked you to come out into the garden because I wish to be alone with you."

Her voice was strange, husky, alluring. Julian forced himself to ignore that. In rising suspicion, he sprang up from the seat.

"Was it Farley? Or perhaps it was Heatherton who put you up to this?" he shouted.

"I don't understand," she said, wincing. "What do you mean?"

"My *friends* have all been placing bets as to when I will fall victim to some beauty's charms. Has one of them sent you to trap me?"

"No," she said emphatically, then put a hand up to her mouth. Her shoulders began to shake, as if she were struggling to hold back tears.

Then he remembered the ordeal she'd just been through. *That* had not been feigned. He sat back down, putting a comforting arm around her. "Oh, I am a brute. Please forgive me."

She stiffened, and seemed even more nervous than before. He released her, but not before he felt that sensation of familiarity again.

"I should be asking *your* forgiveness," she said. "I have lured you out here under false pretenses. However, I assure you it was not on anyone's account but my own."

Julian didn't like to disappoint her, but he didn't dare listen to any more. He thought of Harry, of their wager, and forced himself to rise from the seat again.

"No, please don't leave yet!" There was a hint of desperation in her voice.

Gingerly, he settled himself down on the seat once more, but forced himself to study a nearby statue rather than look back at the beauty at his side.

"I must tell you why I wanted to see you alone," she said. "Will you stay and listen to my story, please?"

He knew it would be wise to leave, but found himself agreeing, against his better judgment.

"I am a widow," she began, and then paused, seeming to gather her courage before continuing.

Julian felt a sweat break out on his forehead. *Please, not a widow!*

"It was an arranged marriage," she continued. "My husband was much older than I. He was a respectable man, but so domineering, and not—not very *affectionate*. Do you understand?"

Almost against his will, he looked at her. Her face was slightly averted, but even in the moonlight he could see her cheeks had reddened with embarrassment.

"Yes, I understand," he said, with feeling. He knew there were men who took their own pleasure, quickly, without a thought for their ladies' comfort or enjoyment. He'd never understand why. Leisurely, playful lovemaking made the final climax all the more worthwhile. But now, when he looked at Diana, lovely, nervous Diana, he found himself seething with rage against the man who had used her so cheaply.

"I have vowed never to marry again," she said. "I cannot bear the thought of being so controlled again by a husband. But I have never known . . . tenderness . . . from a man. And I wish to. I have heard that *you* can be very tender, and . . . kind."

She looked at him, seeming half-frightened, half-hopeful. The slightest breath of a breeze brought her scent to him, sweet and elusive. Lord! What was he going to do? It was if a feast had been placed before him, but he knew he should not partake.

"You know who I am?" he asked, struggling for control.

"Yes," she replied in her mysterious, low voice. "You are Lord Debenham."

"Can you tell me *your* name?" he asked. "Can I see your face?"

"No—please!" she begged, raising a protective hand to her mask.

Diana was so very agitated. Reminding himself again of Harry and the wager, Julian fought down the urge to take her in his arms, and cleared his throat.

"Diana, your husband was a damned fool. You are so beautiful, and you deserve so much better. But this isn't the right place, nor am I the right man. I am sorry, more sorry than I can say. There are reasons why I can't do what you wish. Please understand."

During the earlier part of his speech she had a hopeful expression, but as he concluded, her shoulders began to shake again.

"Oh dear, I knew I could never do this correctly!" she exclaimed, burying her face in her hands.

Damn! He'd made her cry. This was unbearable. He pulled off his helmet, sidled over on the seat, and put his arms around her. He loved how she felt: the warm, velvety skin of her bare arms, the firm-soft feminine body leaning toward him enticingly. She laid her head on his shoulder, but trembled as he gently stroked her shoulders. He ached with the desire to soothe her timidity, and to teach her the pleasures she asked for, pleasures that would surely exceed anything she could possibly imagine.

"Diana, you are irresistible," he said hoarsely.

She raised her head and looked up at him, moonlit eyes glittering strangely through her mask. They seemed to be pleading with him—for what? To be gentle? He would be.

"Don't be afraid. I would never hurt you. Do you believe me?"

She nodded, her lips parted invitingly.

With that, the last shreds of his self-control disappeared.

He bent his head down toward her, and noticed she was holding her breath. She was nervous, and more than ever he was certain it was the first time she'd done anything so bold. He had to make this right. He wouldn't hurt her for the world.

Suddenly he froze. He'd said almost the same thing about Harry.

He released Diana and sprang up from the seat. "I can't do this. I can't!"

"What have I done wrong?" she asked. "Please, tell me what to do and I'll do it. I may never have such a chance again!"

The frantic tone of her voice tore at his insides. He knew if he stayed much longer, he might not be able to stop himself again.

"It's not your fault, but I must go," he said, pacing in front of her as he tried to think of something to ease her distress. "You are very beautiful, and under other circumstances, I would be more than happy to do as you wish. But you see, I already love someone else."

He stopped in his tracks, feeling as if he'd been seared by lightning. He'd blurted out the first excuse he could think of, and it suddenly struck him that it was true.

This wasn't about the wager, or his uncles, or his estate anymore. None of those things mattered if he couldn't have Harry. Ever since he'd come up with the notion of marrying her, he'd been building a picture in his mind of what their life together would be like. How they'd ride, play, and work together. How he would reintroduce her into society and make sure everyone knew exactly what a splendid person she was.

He loved Harry, he realized with a sudden blinding clarity. He probably always had. He couldn't imagine a future without her. And yet he'd almost jeopardized their future, just for a brief passionate encounter with a beautiful stranger.

"Good-bye," he said, taking one last look at Diana. She was sitting perfectly still, and looked pale and fragile. He hated having upset her, but there was nothing he could do to console her now.

He wrenched himself away and ran, plunging down a path at random. He finally stopped when he'd reached the opposite corner of the garden, where another small fountain gurgled. Going up to it, he scooped up a handful of water and splashed it over his face, hoping it would cool him. He sat down on the edge of the fountain, leaning forward and burying his face in his hands.

How could he have come so close to losing control? When so many others had failed, how could this one woman have tempted him almost beyond bearing? But he *had* resisted, he reminded himself. He'd gone away before he'd even kissed Diana, or whoever she was, yet he didn't feel at all victorious. He felt like a scoundrel to have left her in such a way. She was probably crying her eyes out right now.

But it was better this way. He didn't think Diana was really cut out for the dangerous game she had tried to play. Perhaps this incident would convince her to give up her search for a lover, and leave her free to meet a man who would restore her faith in marriage. What was wrong with him, that he felt jealousy at the thought?

He had better concentrate on his feelings for Harry. Instantly, his mind's eye conjured up a vision of her at the stables: flushed, with a bit of straw in her hair, shy and appealing. Suddenly he felt restless with the desire to see her again and show her how he felt, but mingled with his eagerness was a growing sense of guilt and unworthiness. He'd laughed when she had accused him of being a rake, but was she right? Was he really so depraved that he might betray his love for her?

No, he wasn't. He couldn't be. He had vowed he would be a faithful husband to Harry, and so he would be. They would have a perfect marriage; no two people were ever more suited for each other.

As he thought this, however, his confidence wavered. With a pain akin to a blow, he remembered that Harry loved him only as a sister would. She had proposed the wager in the first place, but it was clear she had not dreamed that she might lose. It would be horribly unjust to hold her to their bargain. If she married him, it would have to be of her own free will, because she loved him, too.

It was going to be difficult, but Julian knew what he had to do. Tomorrow, he'd have to release Harry from their bargain. At the same time, he would begin to woo her in earnest. But even as he planned, a painful anxiety shook him. After such a wretched start, what were his chances of success?

Harry sat forlornly in the carriage, swaying and bumping over the long road home.

She'd failed.

She tried not to think about Julian's face as he pulled away, exclaiming that he couldn't kiss her. Afterward, he'd said he loved someone else, but it was clear that was simply an excuse.

She fought back sudden tears. She'd wanted to cry when Julian had run off, but instead she'd snatched up his helmet and run back to the carriage. She cradled the helmet in her lap, remembering how handsome Julian had looked attired as a knight of bygone days. She'd played on his sympathy and aroused his gallantry, but when all was said and done that was not enough. She should have trusted her own instincts, when Lady Dearing had convinced her to take part in this masquerade. She should have known better than to think she had the looks or the skill to lure Julian into dalliance.

She caught herself on another sob. Why was she being so foolish? Perhaps she was just tired, and a little overwrought from the pent-up strain of trying to play such a foreign role. Perhaps it was the thought of what she'd have to do tomorrow. She'd have to ask Julian to release her from their bargain.

A hot tear spilled out onto her cheek. Julian would be very angry. She dreaded that, of course. However, he would eventually forgive her. And wouldn't it be worth bearing his anger, to keep him from ruining his life?

Another tear rolled down, and another, and another. What was wrong with her, that she couldn't hold them back? She couldn't stop thinking of Julian, of how he had looked as he pulled away from her, blurting out polite apologies. Not wanting her.

But she had wanted *him*. It was mad, it was ludicrous, but when he'd finally taken her in his arms, her heart had leapt inside her. She'd forgotten her scheme entirely in anticipation of her first real kiss. Then he'd pulled away.

Her tears stilled suddenly. As the truth finally dawned on her, she drew her cloak around her against a sudden chill that had nothing to do with the warm June night.

She knew now why she had been so apprehensive

about marrying Julian, and why she'd felt so restless and confused for the past few months. In her heart she had feared she would fall in love with him, and now it had happened. The devil of it was that there was nothing she could do to make him love her back.

Seven

Harry's heart was heavy the next morning, as she made her way back home from Nurse's cottage. Lady Dearing's coach had left her off there at about three o'clock. Luckily, Nurse's sight was not what it once was, so she hadn't noticed that Harry's eyes were red-rimmed from crying during the long coach ride. Nurse had just cheerfully insisted on undressing her and tucking her into Nurse's own bed. This morning, she had helped the young woman wash and dry her hair and dress in clothes Harry had left there to change into after the ball.

In her old dress and bonnet, Harry knew she looked quite her dowdy, spinsterish self again. She suspected Cinderella had felt just the same way the day after the ball. Except that Harry knew her prince was coming to see her, and that she was going to refuse his suit for all time.

Today, she would ask Julian to cancel the wager. With any luck, he would be so angry that he would stay away. Hopefully, it would be long enough for her to learn to hide her feelings from him.

She resolutely mastered the impulse to cry again. It would not do to behave like a watering-pot when Julian arrived, or he might suspect her secret. She could at least keep her pride intact.

The path from Nurse's cottage took her through a small wood and ended at the grounds behind her father's house. Harry sighed. The house seemed comforting, quiet and sleepy in the mellow morning sunshine. She could see Aunt Claudia sitting in the garden, but decided against joining her. It would be best if she spent a little time alone, rehearsing what she would say to Julian.

Under cover of several large rhododendron bushes, she passed by her aunt and entered the house by a back entrance. Safely in her room, she sat down at her dressing-table to remove her hat. Her dejection gave way to shock when she looked in the mirror.

Botheration! Streaks of black still showed clearly against her soft brown locks. Nurse's eyes being what they were, she kept no mirror, so neither of them had noticed that they hadn't done a thorough job of washing out the dye.

Harry stared at her reflection for a few dazed seconds, then slapped the bonnet back onto her head. Just in time, for at that moment, Martha, the maid who waited on both her and Aunt Claudia, entered the room.

"Lord Debenham is here to see you, Miss."

"Heavens! What is he doing here so early?" Harry exclaimed, jumping up from her chair in a panic. "What am I to do?"

"I don't understand, Miss. Don't you wish to see His Lordship?" asked Martha, a look of puzzlement on her normally placid face.

"Yes, of course, but I can't—not yet!" she replied, trying to collect her thoughts. "Go tell him to wait. And bring me some hot water. No, there's no time for that! Bring me one of Aunt Claudia's caps."

"One of your aunt's caps? But you don't wear caps, Miss," said Martha, her look of confusion deepening.

"I do now. Hurry, please!"

Martha returned from Aunt Claudia's room with a lace-trimmed cap. Then Harry realized she couldn't exchange her bonnet for the cap with Martha looking on.

"Martha, I am not certain I like this one," she said. "Please fetch me another."

Martha looked at her as if she'd lost her mind. Harry decided it was not far from the truth, and forced herself to suppress the hysterical giggle that rose in her throat.

Hurriedly, she removed her bonnet and put the cap on her head. She tucked her hair up into it, and tied the strings under her chin. Looking into the mirror, she blenched. She'd managed to hide her hair, but she looked dreadful, her pale face and darkly shadowed eyes framed by the fussy, heavily trimmed cap. She looked like a scrawny, overwrought chicken.

"I can't see him like this," she muttered. "I *can't!*"

"Is something the matter, Miss?" said Martha, bustling in with another cap in her hand.

"No, nothing. I have decided this cap will do, after all."

"Are you quite sure, Miss?" asked Martha, still eyeing Harry as she might a madwoman.

Harry nodded. It didn't really matter how ugly she looked. Perhaps it would convince Julian he was well rid of a bad bargain, she thought, searching for a handkerchief.

She blew her nose, squared her shoulders, and went down to the drawing room where Julian was waiting. She found him pacing the room, and felt an ache rise in her throat at the sight of him. He turned, and she saw that his face looked haggard. She wondered how long he'd stayed at the ball after she'd left. He didn't look as if he'd slept at all. His expression seemed hungry as he gazed at her, but then it gave way to a look of concern.

"Harry, are you well?" he asked.

"Yes, perfectly," she replied. "Oh, I see you are looking at my cap. I have decided that I have reached the age where I should start wearing them."

"You are only three and twenty!" He gave the cap another puzzled look. "I suppose you know best," he added awkwardly.

They sat down on the sofa where they had sat together so many evenings when he'd visited. Only now, a strange silence fell between them as Harry struggled to summon up the courage to make her speech.

"There is something I have to say to you," said Julian, just as she said the same words.

They both laughed, in embarrassment, and Harry realized that Julian seemed no more comfortable than she.

"You first," he said.

"No, you start," she said, grateful for any delay.

"Harry, I want to release you from our wager. I can't hold you to it. It was a silly idea for me to ever propose to you in such a way."

It seemed that Julian himself had finally seen the wisdom in what she'd been saying about his plan. She should be relieved; now there was no need to ask him to release her. Instead, she felt more wretched than before.

She struggled to find the right words to thank him, but they caught in her throat.

"Please let me finish," he said, and took her hands in his. "I still wish to marry you, more than anything I've ever wanted."

"You don't have to say that," she replied, trying to look cheerful. "I know everyone thinks we are engaged, but I can cry off, and no one will blame you."

"I don't care what everyone thinks," he said. "I just want to marry *you.*"

Oh, why did he have to sound so earnest, and so totally charming?

"It's best that we don't," she said. Gently, she tried to pull her hands back, but he held them firmly. Despite herself, she felt warmed by the touch.

"Harry, you must realize by now that I can be faithful. Do you think I haven't encountered any temptation?" Julian asked, in a serious tone. He paused a few moments before continuing. "I probably shouldn't tell you, but perhaps when you hear this you'll believe me. Last night, I went to a masquerade, and met a . . . well, a very charming, very exquisite lady."

Harry felt her heart begin to pound at his description. He'd found Diana *charming? Exquisite?* "What happened?"

"She told me she was looking for a lover," said Julian, looking troubled. "I must be honest with you, Harry. She tempted me, more than I've ever been tempted before. I was going to kiss her, and then I just couldn't."

Somehow, Harry found her lips had gone dry. She licked them, and managed to croak out the question, "Why?"

"I couldn't bear the thought of losing *you.* Harry, I promise I'll stay here in Kent with you always. We need never go back to London, or anywhere else. Just say you'll marry me!"

"You would make such a sacrifice? Just to marry

me? Why?" she asked, not wanting to hope, but unable to stop herself.

"Because I love you!"

She stared at him. If her heart was pounding before, it was galloping now.

"I know you still think of me as a friend, perhaps even as a brother. But, Harry, we are not brother and sister. Your feelings might change, if you let them. Will you try?"

She gazed into his eyes. She'd never seen them blaze with such emotion. For *her?*

"You don't believe that I love you?" he cried. "I'll prove it to you!"

Before she could say anything, he closed the distance between them and pulled her into his arms. Then he bent his head down and kissed her. At first he merely pressed his lips fervently against hers. She sat rigidly within the circle of his arms, still not quite believing what was happening, and without any notion of how she should respond. Then the reality of the situation struck her. She looked tired and hideous, but Julian was kissing her anyway!

The unexpected joy of it all set her pulses leaping anew, and she twined her arms around him and hugged him back with all her might. He tightened his hold, and she gave a little moan. His tongue teased her lips apart, and began to warmly explore her mouth. She stiffened again at the shock of it. She'd never imagined a kiss could be like this.

Then a warmth spread through her like nothing she'd ever felt before. Instinctively, she began to follow his lead, and their tongues curled about each other in a strange, wonderful embrace that hinted at even greater pleasures yet to come.

As he kissed Harry, Julian couldn't stop marveling at his good fortune. She must love him, or she would not be responding to his kiss with such innocent fervor. It was clear she'd never been kissed before, but she was definitely doing her best to make up for lost time. He felt nearly insane with the yearning to touch and caress every part of her, but he forced himself to be careful, not to shock her too much.

He finally withdrew from her lips, and heard a little gasp of disappointment as he kissed her cheek. He wanted to kiss her ear, but her blasted cap was in the way, so he moved down her neck, and found places there just as sweet. He followed the lovely line of her neck down to where the little hollow at the base of her throat was just barely revealed by her modest décolletage. He kissed her there, hungrily, thrilling to feel the quick beat of her heart, reveling in her scent, mysterious and innocently sweet at the same time. Her scent . . .

Lilies of the valley.

Abruptly he pulled back, assailed by a fantastic, unbelievable suspicion. He gazed into her eyes. They were dazed and darkened with passion, and he realized that looking into them was destroying his ability to think rationally. Instead, he focused on her cap. Her cap . . .

He released her and jumped up from the sofa. "What are you hiding underneath that cap, Harry?" he asked, swallowing a painful tightness in his throat.

She was still staring at him, but now fear and remorse were written all over her face. He could see tears forming in the corners of her eyes, and tried to ignore them. If only he were not so affected by the sight of feminine tears!

She managed to hold her tears back, except for one

which rolled down one cheek. He found himself longing to kiss it dry, and realized he was a complete fool.

"Where were you last night?" he growled. "The truth now, please."

"I see you have guessed," she said in a still, quiet voice. "I attended your cousin's masquerade, dressed as the goddess Diana. I'm so sorry. I never wanted to deceive you so."

"It was all a trick, wasn't it? To make me lose the bet. I never dreamed you thought marriage with me would be so terrible that you would go to such lengths to avoid it!"

"I did it for your sake, too," she retorted. "I didn't want you to commit yourself to a marriage before you found someone you could truly love."

"Thank you!" he said sarcastically.

She winced, and another tear rolled down her cheek. His anger faded to a tired sort of bitterness.

"Couldn't you have just asked me to let you out of the bargain, instead of making such a fool of me?" he asked, more gently. "You know I wouldn't have forced you into marrying me."

"I knew how disappointed you would be. I couldn't bear the thought of losing your friendship over this. I thought it would be better to prove to you that you should wait until you met the right lady. I never meant to make a fool of you. Please forgive me!"

Julian felt a dull ache settle in his chest. It was clear that even if she'd enjoyed their kiss, Harry didn't love him and probably never would. Part of him longed to heal the breach between them, but his disappointment was still too raw.

"I had better go," he said, turning to leave the room.

"No, wait!" said Harry, a pleading tone in her voice.

Out of the corner of his eye, he saw her get up from the sofa.

He stopped, wanting to refuse but unable to do so.

"Julian, when you didn't kiss me last night, I was miserable."

"Of course. Because your precious scheme failed," he said, still looking the other way.

"No, because I truly wanted you to kiss me."

At that, he turned back around. She looked so nervous, and in deadly earnest.

"Oh, Julian, until last night I didn't know that I loved you. I think I always have. Please forgive me."

He forced himself to stay calm as she came to him and put her arms awkwardly around him.

"I *do* love you," she said in a husky voice that reminded him of last night's encounter.

He looked down into her eyes, and saw that they were bright with tears. A smile trembled about her lips, and he finally realized that she spoke the truth. By some miracle, her feelings had undergone the same transformation as his!

He realized he'd been holding his breath, and released it suddenly. He put his arms around her and pulled her closer.

"Very well, then," he said gruffly. "I'll forgive you."

"You will?" she asked, looking adorably flustered.

"On three conditions, that is," he said, unable to resist a mischievous impulse.

"No!" she exclaimed. "No more bargains. No more conditions."

"Don't worry, you goose! I think you won't find my conditions at all unreasonable," he said, with a reassuring smile.

"Very well, then. What are they?"

"First, you must marry me."

"Yes, Julian," she said meekly. "And?"

He kissed her briefly. "Second, you must promise never to wear that ugly cap again."

She giggled, and nodded. "What is your third condition?"

"You will have to indulge me on this one," he warned.

"Tell me. What is it?"

"You must promise that once we are married, you'll wear that goddess costume now and again."

She laughed, blushing, then tilted her head up to kiss him.

Harry's father and aunt received the news of the engagement with placid satisfaction, making Harry wonder if they had realized she and Julian had been fated to be together all along. Not long after, Lady Dearing arrived, and professed herself overjoyed at the news.

The day being so fine, they all convened for a luncheon on the terrace. At a convenient moment, Lady Dearing took a seat beside Harry and begged to know all the details of what had transpired at the ball and afterward. By the time Harry finished her recital, Lady Dearing's eyes were sparkling with mingled joy and amusement.

"This is so much better even than what I had intended!" she exclaimed.

"So you planned it all just to bring us together?" asked Harry.

"Of course, dear. One would have to have been a fool not to have seen how much in love you were, and I am *not* a fool. You both merely needed to be made aware of your affection for each other. Mind you, I did expect Debenham to kiss you at the masquerade, but this is even better, for now he has proven how much he loves you."

Harry smiled, and thanked Lady Dearing for all her help. "Perhaps you will think me impertinent, but may I ask you something?" she added.

"Of course," said Lady Dearing with a smile.

"That story you told me to tell Julian—about being a widow, I mean. That is *your* story, is it not?"

After a moment, Lady Dearing nodded, her smile fading a little. But she didn't seem offended, so Harry persisted.

"I am so fortunate, I hate to think of anyone else giving up hope of finding such happiness. I hope you are not truly set against marriage?"

"I find meddling in other people's lives much more amusing," said Lady Dearing. She spoke lightly, but Harry thought she detected a fleeting look of regret in Lady Dearing's eyes. The next instant, however, they were dancing again. Harry sensed she could pry no further.

"I am so glad you meddled in ours," she said.

"Oh, pish! I only sped things up a trifle. You were well on your way ever since you and Debenham devised your little wager. Remember, it was his idea to marry you in the first place. He may not have realized that he loved you, but somehow he must have known you were meant for each other."

Harry saw Julian coming toward them. Feeling that new, wonderful quickening of her heart again at the sight of him, she realized that Lady Dearing had spoken nothing but the truth.

* * *

Julian had to force himself to keep from pacing as he awaited Harry's arrival at their small parish church. He had barely seen her in the last two weeks. After acquiring the special license allowing them to marry quickly, he had busied himself with making sure Ardleigh Court was ready for his new bride. Meanwhile, Lady Dearing had spirited Harry off to London to revel in shopping for bride-clothes. The one time he and Harry had managed a few moments alone for a kiss had left him only hungrier than ever to make her his own.

Finally he heard footsteps, and looked toward the doorway. For an instant, Harry and her father were silhouetted against the bright sunshine outside. Then they moved forward, and Julian could have sworn his heart stopped beating for an instant at the sight of his bride.

A little lace veil left the front of her hair free, revealing feathery little curls all about her face. Bemused, Julian realized her hair had been cut quite short, and the *gamine* style was a perfect frame for her delicate features.

She held a posy of summer flowers in rose and blue, and her ivory dress was trimmed with pale blue satin ribbon that brought out the blue in her eyes. The tiny, tantalizing bodice clung to her bosom; the skirt flowed gracefully over a figure that seemed even more willowy and enticing than what he remembered from the masquerade. But this was no masquerade. She was still Harry, and she would soon be *his* Harry.

She came beside him, and he sighed, realizing he'd been holding his breath at the sight of her. She smiled shyly up at him, as if uncertain of the effect she had on him. He smiled back, feeling a joy and expectation like none he'd ever felt before.

Warmed by Julian's smile, knowing she was surrounded by a small, loving group of family and friends, Harry composed herself and listened to the vicar speaking the words of the service. Soon, he prompted Julian to make his vow.

"Wilt thou have this woman to be thy wedded wife, to live together after God's ordinance in the holy estate of Matrimony? Wilt thou love her, comfort her, honor, and keep her in sickness and in health; and, forsaking all others, keep thee only unto her, as long as ye both shall live?"

"I will," said Julian, and Harry thrilled to hear his voice ringing out boldly through the small church.

When it was her turn, she found her own voice was quite steady, her earlier nervousness having vanished at the sight of Julian's ardent smile.

Before long, the church bell was ringing, and Julian led her outside into the breezy day filled with sunshine, holding her close to his side. She leaned joyfully against him as he tossed coins to the children waiting in the churchyard.

Just a short time ago, she would never have imagined she would marry Julian. Now it felt utterly, perfectly right. No other couple could possibly know each other as well as they did, and yet recent events had proven they still had much to learn about each other. It was going to be delightful.

She would even wager on it!

A PICTURE PERFECT ROMANCE

Alice Holden

One

Sir Nigel Westhaven poured his best port into the three crystal goblets which rested on a silver tray that his daughter Phillipa had set onto the low sofa table earlier.

"Did you find Lord Charing in good health?" he asked Lord Darrington, his son Harry's houseguest, as he handed the dark-haired viscount a glass of wine.

"Yes, Vienna agrees with my father," Lord Darrington said. He seated his tall frame into a green upholstered chair, his broad back to the drawing room window that overlooked Brookfield's gardens. He twirled the stem of his glass between his long, slender fingers and studied the eddying wine rather morosely.

"His Lordship ordered me to come home to England and hare myself off to London to find a wife. I am to accomplish this after I meet with the estate manager at Fairlea to ascertain if all is as it should be." He glanced toward Harry, who sat in a wing chair, a drop-leaf table separating them. He hoped for a word of sympathy, but gained only an inane smile from his best friend.

From the green-and-white-striped sofa which faced the window, Sir Nigel winked across the room at his blond, brown-eyed son, who was a younger version of himself. Then he looked once again at Lord Darrington.

"Why the long face, lad?" he said to the viscount. "Since Lord Charing has now joined the ranks of the diplomats, he needs a family member to keep an eye on Fairlea. No matter how efficient your manager might be, he does not have the proprietary interest in the estate that a Roarke would have. As for the other matter, at twenty-nine a gentleman has a duty to marry and set up his nursery." Without warning, Sir Nigel turned his full attention from Lord Darrington to the window where his elderly gardener had appeared among the flower beds.

Harry pulled a face at his father's sudden impolite distraction. "What Sir Nigel is getting at, Devon, is that I am to be married."

His Lordship, who had been plain Devon Roarke to Harry since their boyhood days at Eton, yelped, "You are getting leg-shackled?"

Harry smiled indulgently at his flabbergasted friend, while Sir Nigel took his eyes briefly from the gardener and let out a booming laugh. "It is not a tragedy, my boy, but a desirable circumstance."

Devon developed a sheepish grin. "What a lackwit I am. Of course it is. But, Harry, why did you not write me of the happy event?"

"It has been but a fortnight since I decided that I could not live without her."

Devon raised his glass in a toast. "Congratulations, Harry. Do I know the young lady?"

"No, Dev," Harry said. "I met her after you left for the Continent. Claudia, for that is her name, came to stay with Mrs. Emerson, her paternal grandmother, on an adjoining estate. This occurred after she was orphaned at the death of her father in London several months ago."

Devon flashed him a smile. "I look forward to meeting the lady who has finally captured your heart."

"You will this evening. She joins us for dinner." Harry's voice lost some of its enthusiasm. "Unfortunately, her grandmother won't allow a formal betrothal until a lengthy mourning period has passed."

Sir Nigel, whose attention had never fully left the caretaker in the yard, bounced to his feet.

"Damme, you must excuse me, lads, but Joseph has fetched his clippers. He will become unnecessarily ruthless with his pruning unless I stop him."

Devon arched a brow and followed Sir Nigel with his eyes until Harry's father vanished into the hall. Once he was certain the older man was out of earshot, he said, "What the devil was that all about?"

Harry snorted. "Over the years my father has turned into an inveterate agriculturist, protective of every tree, shrub, and flower on the estate. You saw how he attires himself in rough country clothes and sturdy workman's boots. He joins Joseph, the gardener, digging and weeding as if he, too, were out to hire."

"Surely, you don't object to such a harmless avocation if he is content," Devon said, bewildered by Harry's inflated reproof.

"Dash it all! He has made a religion of his puttering and has become so engrossed in his own pursuits that he is blind to Pip's condition."

"Pip?"

"My sister Phillipa. It's a nickname she has carried since babyhood."

"Ah yes, Miss Westhaven. Is she ill?" Devon had taken little notice of the lady when they had been introduced, but, from what he could recall, she had appeared to be in the pink of health.

"Not ill, but on the road to spinsterhood. I think she gave up all thoughts of marriage after Cedric Baines took a fatal ball in the Channel some four years ago during a minor skirmish with a French frigate."

Devon leaned forward. "Not the Cedric Baines who was two years ahead of us in school?"

"The same. He was a naval officer, you know."

"I didn't know," Devon said, taken aback. "Baines was so bookish and ill-suited to a military profession. I always saw his future as that of a university don."

"Would that he had been so inclined. He would be alive today, and Pip would be his wife, not withering on the vine."

Perceiving that Harry's tone clearly-spoke of self-pity rather than concern for his sister or the fallen sailor, Devon said, "What is your quarrel with Sir Nigel?"

"He has not lifted a finger to remedy Phillipa's situation. I ask you, Devon, should not a caring father be casting round for a suitable husband for his daughter?"

Devon took a sip of wine and regarded Harry thoughtfully. "Come on, Harry. What is this *really* all about?" he said.

Harry threw up his hands. "Damn it, Dev. Not only is Mrs. Emerson thwarting me, but Phillipa is, too."

"Edify me," Devon said, prepared to listen, for he had never known Harry to get worked up over nothing.

"The servants here are so much in Phillipa's pocket that I find even when I give an order, they go behind my back and seek her approval."

Devon shrugged, dismissing this explanation as a specious reason for Harry's distress. "You are seldom around and haven't been at Brookfield much since you left for school years ago. I don't think you and I engender trust with the people on our estates, who see us as London dandies. You know, that is one reason I sent Ransome ahead of me to Fairlea," he said, speaking of his valet, "to give them fair warning. I did not want to drop in unannounced and have the servants and workers think I was trying to catch them out letting down on their duties."

"But you don't have a domineering, efficient sister in control. Phillipa will make Claudia's life miserable after we wed and take up residence here at Brookfield. My bride won't be able to cope with Pip, who has had the run of the household since my mother died six years ago. Lud, Devon, my little love has just turned eighteen and is gentle raised. What chance would she have against Phillipa, who flouts even my directives? Since I have been here, my sister has sent me into a pelter more than once, countermanding my orders and replacing them with her own."

Devon spent a moment collecting his thoughts after listening to Harry's long, emotional outburst.

"It seems the only solution to your problem is for Miss Westhaven to marry and remove to her husband's home," he said at last.

"Exactly! That is what I have been trying to make you understand!"

The drawing room door was thrust open and the thorn in Harry's side breezed in. Devon rose from his chair in deference to the presence of a female; he studied Miss Westhaven with new interest after having listened to Harry's complaints.

Devon considered himself a connoisseur of women, having spent better than a decade observing the young ladies who were the cream of London society, as well as having had a number of high flyers under his protection.

He decided that he would not have taken a second look at Miss Westhaven had he encountered her in the drawing rooms of the *ton*. The chit lacked style. Her brown fly-away hair was an unholy mess. Despite her symmetrical features and large brown eyes, in his opinion, she had a forgettable face. Her shapeless gown lacked any adornment, even the simplest lace, and belonged in a church poor box. Sadly, Harry was going to have a devil of a time finding a suitable gentleman to take such an Antidote off his hands.

Phillipa would have died of mortification had she been aware of the viscount's harsh conception of her. On her part, she found Lord Darrington, who was dressed to the nines in a well-fitted maroon coat and black breeches, very dashing.

She fingered a dark gray button on her collarless dress and apologized to her brother for interrupting him.

"I saw Papa working in the yard with Joseph and assumed that you and Lord Darrington had finished your wine as well. I shall come back later."

She made to turn around, but Harry got to his feet and said, "Stay, Phillipa. I was about to suggest to Devon that we go to the stables. I want to show him the bay I purchased at Tattersall's last month."

"A new horse?" Devon said. "Splendid." He faced Phillipa to thank her for the refreshments. "My compliments to the cook. The wine cakes were delicious."

She acknowledged his civility with a smile. "I have seen to a valet for you, my lord, since you have sent your man on to Fairlea."

Before Devon could express his appreciation for her consideration, Harry said, "You will find Basil quite acceptable, Devon. He does for me whenever I come home. He is not Ransome, but then who is." Devon was kind enough to share his highly proficient valet with Harry whenever they abided together in London.

Phillipa knew with an uncomfortable certainty that her next words would bring an explosive retort from Harry, but she plunged ahead recklessly.

"James Newell is going to see to the viscount's needs."

"What?" Harry roared precisely as Phillipa had anticipated. "James is not a valet. He is a gawky boy. See that Basil serves His Lordship."

Phillipa had become a champion of James Newell's unconcealed dream to become a valet. She was not about to succumb submissively to Harry's arrogant command.

"Basil has other duties," she said, her chin climbing a notch. "Besides, he is no more a personal servant than James, but a man-of-all-work. James, at least, *wants* to be a valet."

"James is a corkbrain. Let him practice on someone else, not a lord of the realm."

Devon could see that an unpleasant scene between the siblings was building. Miss Westhaven appeared to be as bullheaded as Harry. In a move to avoid a donnybrook without taking sides, he claimed, "It hardly matters who does for me in the two days I will be here. I can as well do for myself."

"I wouldn't hear of it, my lord," Phillipa said, speaking to the viscount, but challenging Harry with her resolute brown eyes and a mouth set in an uncompromising fashion. "I have already freed James to look after you. Basil has other duties."

Harry fumed; his hands at his sides clenched into

fists, but he yielded. "Have it your way, madam. There is nothing new in that." He spun on the heels of his smart top boots and stamped from the room.

Lord Darrington followed Harry under Phillipa's gaze. What a good-looking man the viscount was, with wonderful blue eyes, dark where Harry was fair, but almost as handsome as her brother; at two or three inches taller, he was a bit more imposing.

Lord Darrington turned at the doorway and regarded her before disappearing. He had elevated his shoulders slightly in an undecipherable shrug that could have been an apology or embarrassment at being caught in the middle or . . . who knew the vagaries of men? Phillipa thought as she collected the wine carafe, the attendant goblets, and the remaining wine cakes.

Take Harry, for instance, she mused. For years he had come home periodically and seemed perfectly amenable. He had never interfered with her management of the household and had taken no interest in the manner in which she allocated duties among the small staff of servants. He had been perfectly content with the comforts she had provided for him without the crotchets and quirks that had, lately, led him on a fault-finding frenzy.

Removing a dust cloth from her pocket, Phillipa wiped the tables and picked up the tray she had loaded. Shaking her head, she headed for the kitchen, puzzled by the mysterious peculiarities of the male brain.

Two

Devon studied the framed charcoal sketches of Phillipa at age one, and Harry at six, on the dining room wall. He was waiting with Sir Nigel for the others to assemble for dinner.

"Who executed these drawings?" he asked.

"An itinerant artist," Sir Nigel said. "He appeared one day with a band of gypsies who camped by the river. Since the man wanted only a pittance, I had them done."

Devon had been drawing since his nursemaid-governess had first put a pencil into his hand to teach him to write. He had drawn pictures even before he had printed his alphabet and had never lost his love of sketching.

The artist who had drawn the children had used good charcoal that had obviously been purchased from an art dealer. He had taken the time to properly fix his portraits into a permanent state, which was essential for charcoal sketches.

Devon himself had worked extensively in the media. He said, "The results are quite good for a traveling artist."

Sir Nigel nodded. "I always thought so," he declared, but turned from the viscount and consigned his full attention to his daughter, who had entered the room. She walked over to the two men.

"Harry and Claudia should be here at any minute," Phillipa said. "I heard the carriage wheels on the drive as I came downstairs."

Phillipa raised a brow, not knowing what to make of it, when Devon Roarke left off looking at the childhood pictures and stared silently at her blue silk gown. She had first worn the dress at an assembly years ago; it had been the night before Cedric Baines had left for the naval assignment from which he had never returned. The play of the viscount's cool, assessing eyes over the swell of her bosom and the curves of her hips made her nervous. His hard gaze could only have lasted a few seconds, but it seemed an eternity to her.

But to Phillipa's relief, his critical perusal moved from her seasons-old frock to Harry, when her brother came through the door. With Claudia on his arm, he announced, "Here we are."

Standing to the side, Phillipa watched Lord Darrington being introduced to Harry's doll-like bride-to-be. He smiled with obvious admiration at Claudia Emerson, who was exceedingly pretty with satin black hair and big violet eyes.

Phillipa waited a reasonable interval for the viscount to pay homage to Claudia's many favorable attributes and congratulate Harry on his good fortune in winning the little charmer for his own. Then she took charge and seated everyone at the table and motioned for Basil to fill the plates from the sideboard.

No man could be expected to be immune to Claudia's beauty, Phillipa thought. Yet, it was not flattering to be inspected as if one were an exotic insect under glass while Harry's love was lavished with wild encomiums.

She had never been one to fish for compliments, but Phillipa wished that Lord Darrington could have shown a spark of gallantry; he ought to have bestowed at least a single word of praise on her, however insincere he might have been.

Basil carried out his duties with quiet proficiency during the genteel, innocuous conversation which was exchanged around the table. The servant uncorked a bottle of burgundy. While he poured wine into each diner's glass, Sir Nigel asked about the younger gentlemen's upcoming trip to London.

Phillipa listened to the viscount reveal that Harry would be stopping with him at Lord Charing's town house in Grosvenor Square.

"As you know, my father is still abroad," he said, "so we will have the run of the house."

During the meal, Phillipa was very aware of Lord Darrington sitting beside her. His spicy cologne permeated the air in her vicinity. His hand was so close to hers, that if she moved her fingers six inches to the left, she would be touching his skin.

Wrapped in her own daydreams, Phillipa had let the table talk flow around her, paying scant attention until her mind was wrenched back to the moment. She realized with a start that something was wrong.

She came fully to her senses and met Harry's black look from across the table. "We all know that Pip casts us all in the shade with her efficiency, but I believe Claudia and I will be up to the task of running Brookfield."

Phillipa gazed at Harry, perplexed by his words. Meeting only a tight-lipped hardness, she turned to her father for some elucidation.

Sir Nigel was calmly picking bones from a piece of fish.

"Who said you wouldn't be? I merely wanted to reassure you that you need not rush to take over your estate duties when I said that Pip does a superb job of keeping the accounts and dealing with the bailiff. She runs the household as smoothly as your mother ever did."

Claudia laid a beseeching hand on Harry's coat sleeve. "Grandmama herself has said I have much to learn about keeping a house," she said, her voice sweet and childlike.

"That may be," Harry retorted, "but I certainly can keep the books and deal with a bailiff."

Phillipa felt sorry for the young woman, who seemed upset by Harry's backlash.

"I shall be here to help you, Miss Emerson," she said, kindly, in a sincere effort to placate Claudia.

Harry continued to glower at Phillipa as if she had made matters worse. Completely at a loss, she stared at her wineglass.

Sir Nigel finished the last morsel of fish on his plate and asked Phillipa which of the servants had caught the trout.

"James Newell," she said, raising her head to meet his eyes.

Opportunely, Lord Darrington jumped in with a fish story and soon the awkward moment was smoothed over. Phillipa was relieved to see that Harry had covered Claudia's hand with his own and was smiling down at her. But she could hardly wait for the day to arrive when he would return to London. She had had quite enough of her impossible brother's bad temper.

* * *

After her usual morning walk the next day, Phillipa came through the back door and stepped into the kitchen. She smiled as she recalled the chaotic scene on the porch when she had left earlier.

James Newell had been polishing Lord Darrington's tasseled Hessians when Basil appeared and said to the blond young man, "I heard His Lordship stirring when I was upstairs moments ago. You had best get his boots up to him, or he will be forced to go about in his slippers."

James had leapt to his feet and snatched up the Hessians and some brown riding boots. Clutching both pairs of footwear to his chest, he'd dashed past Basil, while muttering some very colorful words.

Basil had pinned a disparaging eye on the tins of polish and the brushes strewn over the steps. He had shaken his head. "That nodcock will never be a gentleman's valet."

"He is young yet," Phillipa had said in defense of James, who was a month shy of his nineteenth birthday.

Her smile at the memory dwindled as she hung her black shawl on a wooden peg. She untied the faded ribbons of the flat broad-brimmed straw, removed the hat from her clubbed-together brown hair, and set it on a shelf.

Cook was rolling out dough for pies on a scrubbed wooden table while Dora, who was Basil's female counterpart of all work, swished around a bar of brown soap in a dishpan in the sink.

"I see Mr. Harry and Lord Darrington have had their breakfast," Phillipa said when the maid began to pile the gentlemen's dirty plates and coffee cups into the soapy dishwater.

"Yes, Miss Pip, I cleared the table not ten minutes

ago," Dora replied. "I could use a fresh supply of towels."

"I will get them for you," Phillipa said and went off to the linen press in the hall. As she lifted the cupboard's latch, she was startled to hear Harry's voice coming from the small sitting room beyond the common wall.

"But, you can see now, Dev, why I am at my wit's end. Claudia is shy and soft-spoken and no match for my aggressive sister. Even in the best of cases two mistresses in one household is one too many, but in my situation it would be disastrous. Phillipa needs a husband of her own. But what am I to do? The provoking creature has made no effort to find one."

Phillipa chewed on the edge of her lower lip. Her heart sank. Harry did not want her living at Brookfield once he and Claudia were married. She reached for the kitchen towels, but Devon Roarke's voice stopped her hand in midair.

"You know, Harry, the situation is not going to be rosy for Miss Westhaven, either."

"What do you mean?" Harry said.

"When you are master of Brookfield and have full authority over her, you do not plan to leave the disbursement of funds in her hands?"

"I'm no addlepate. Of course not!"

"Then think about it, Harry. Miss Westhaven will be dependent on you for everything; even the food which passes her lips, and every scrap of clothing on her back, not to mention pin money which you may or may not want to give her. She will become that dreaded unmarried female who ends up a burden on her family and the scorn of society. A woman with a personality as strong as Miss Westhaven's will find her situation intolerable."

"Dash it all, Dev. Pip is my sister. I don't want to humiliate her; I just want her to find fulfillment in a good husband. She should remove to his house and leave Claudia and me in peace."

Phillipa had heard enough. She peeled off half a dozen towels from a larger stack and closed the door quietly.

She was a little numb, but not really angry with Harry, only hurt that he had not been candid with her. She was not an unreasonable person, contrary to what he thought. He did have some good arguments for her removal on his side. But it was Lord Darrington's picture of a bleak future that really sobered her. She knew that every word the viscount had said was true. It was exactly like that for too many unwanted female relatives, who were forced to exist on the charity of their families.

In the kitchen, she handed the towels to Dora and dressed herself once again in the black shawl and decrepit hat. She put her hand in the pocket of her brown dress and removed a book which was weighing down her skirt. She had intended to find some time to read more of it, but what she needed now was to be alone to think. She carried the book with her, for she did not dare leave it lying around.

"Are you going out again, Miss Pip?" the maid asked.

"Yes, Dora. I shall be in the chapel garden if you need me."

Three

Devon was ambling around the estate grounds when he spied Phillipa sliding through a narrow access cut into a thick hedge. Wondering what was behind the high natural fence through which she had disappeared, he followed her.

Phillipa had settled herself on a stone bench under a shade tree when she noticed the viscount coming toward her. She quickly rammed the book she held deep into the pocket of her plain brown skirt and watched his approach. He looked smart, dressed for riding in a dark green coat, tan breeches, and brown boots.

She had come to the sequestered garden to be alone and to consider a plan, which had come to her out of the blue, to go to London to seek a husband. The last thing she wanted was company.

But she was to have no choice, for when the viscount came up to her, he sat down beside her on the stone seat without an invitation. He looked around him.

"What an enchanting site," he said, taking in the place that was Phillipa's favorite spot on the estate.

An impenetrable wall of rhododendron bushes cloistered the garden in beauty and peaceful isolation. Surrounding flower beds were filled with early spring blooms. The bench where the two of them sat was in the front yard of a quaint stone church. The sun bounced off the stained glass windows and shone on a polished wooden cross on the spire.

"Is this where Harry and Claudia will be married?" he asked. "The chapel would be perfect for a small wedding."

Looking back over her shoulder at the ivy-covered church, Phillipa said, "I think so, too. June would be the prettiest, for it is when my father's pink and white roses are in full bloom. However, Mrs. Emerson wants her granddaughter to be wed in the village church, where she herself was married over fifty years ago and where Claudia's parents had their nuptials."

The viscount flicked some imaginary dust from his boot top. "Did you plan to marry Cedric Baines here?" he asked.

"You knew Cedric?"

"I knew him, but not well. Harry mentioned your connection with him and of his unfortunate demise. I was sorry to hear of it."

Her love affair with the young lieutenant had been sweet and brief and remained a sad memory; even so, Phillipa had no lingering unresolved grief which would have kept her from speaking forthrightly about her former suitor.

"Cedric was planning to leave the Navy in November for a teaching post at Harrow. We would have married in December before the new term began in January. The chapel is not heated and would have been too cold at that time of year and, of course, the garden would have been barren. There are no flowers blooming in winter, and the trees are bare of leaves. No, my lord, we would not have wed here, but in the village church, too."

Devon nodded and stretched his neck toward the sky.

"I hope this beautiful weather holds for another day. I would not like to get rained on. I am on horseback since I sent my valet ahead in the travel coach to prepare for my visit to Fairlea," he said, repeating what Phillipa already knew.

"You are leaving in the morning, then," she stated, since Harry had not mentioned Lord Darrington's actual departure time.

"Yes, Newell has started packing for me. He insisted, but I fear Ransome has exacting standards and will have something to say when he unpacks what young Mr. Newell has wrought."

His voice held only the gentlest mockery, but Phillipa took the implied criticism to heart. "Oh dear, I suppose I should have listened to Harry and let Basil look after you."

"Don't overset yourself, Miss Westhaven," he said, matter-of-factly. "No harm done. But, the lad has much to learn."

"Is there no hope for James? Above all things he wants to be a gentleman's valet."

"There is always hope, ma'am. The lad is likeable and industrious. He would probably progress under the tutelage of an experienced man."

Devon reflected on Miss Westhaven's dull, serviceable dress and wondered why she insisted on wearing concealing robes. Last night she had stunned him into speechlessness when she had appeared in a dated, form-fitting silk gown which revealed that she had a rather nice body.

Phillipa, unaware that her figure was being admired in a small way, was still thinking about James. "Perhaps I could buy some books on the subject that he could study or from which I could help him learn."

"I'm afraid not. No such books exist, at least none that I am aware of. Valeting is one of those on-the-job things," Devon replied with a marked lack of interest in Newell, visualizing instead the curvy hips and full breasts hidden beneath Miss Westhaven's ugly clothes. But the word *book* revived an earlier curiosity.

"But speaking of books," he said to that end, "what book are you hiding in your pocket? Even from a distance I could see you hurriedly stash it away as I approached."

Phillipa sat a little straighter. "I am not hiding anything," she claimed in a rather small voice. "It's just a book. Shakespeare."

Detecting a guilty flush on her cheeks, Devon said, "Shakespeare, eh? Let's have a look."

Phillipa was so startled when he peremptorily snatched the book from her pocket that she never thought to stop him. After the fact, she gasped her protest. "Give that back to me, sir. You have no right . . ."

But the viscount's long arm held the book high over his head and beyond her reach as he read the title.

"Damme," he swore, his smiling face darkening into a hard scowl. "Where did you get this rubbish?"

"It is none of your affair," Phillipa said, heatedly. "Now give it back this instant, sir."

"*A Vindication of the Rights of Woman,*" he said, scornfully. "You dishonor your mother by reading such a subversive tome."

"Subversive?" Phillipa's voice squeaked indignantly. "Why? Because Mary Wollstonecraft writes that women should have rights equal to that of men? What is so terrible about advocating a comparable education for both sexes?"

"That is not the worst of it and you know it," he

said, his own voice rising in righteous indignation. "The singularly licentious Wollstonecraft would have made lightskirts of decent women."

"Granted some of her views are outré. Clearly, I would never go so far as to advocate living in sin," Phillipa said, judiciously.

"How noble of you." One corner of the viscount's mouth curled into a sneer that made the ones Harry bestowed on her look like friendly smiles, but Phillipa stood her ground.

"But that does not negate the parts that are fair. For instance, why must a husband be allowed to control his wife's every action without her having any say?"

"Nonsense. A wife has all sorts of freedom. She has the running of the house. She can pay calls and receive callers at will and attend functions unescorted."

"As long as she parrots her master's voice and remains submissive and docile," Phillipa huffed.

The viscount sniffed. "I would bet a pony you were not forthcoming with these corrupt ideas when Cedric Baines courted you, else the man would have run for his life. Any sensible man would."

"I would not have hidden my true feelings from Lieutenant Baines. He was not so narrow-minded." Phillipa knew she was parsing the truth, for Cedric, after all, was a man and would have been no less shocked than Lord Darrington that she had purchased and read the notorious work.

The viscount smiled nastily. "Why did you find it necessary to say you were reading Shakespeare if you were not ashamed of possessing that misguided female's work?"

Phillipa longed to slap the smug look from the viscount's arrogant face, but, at that moment, she saw Harry coming through the fence. She panicked.

"Give me the book," she cried and latched onto one corner of the volume. "Please! Please, sir!" She pulled mightily, but Lord Darrington's viselike grip was immovable.

In the struggle, Phillipa's black shawl slid from her shoulders, and her straw hat tilted onto her back, hanging by its faded ribbons from her neck.

The viscount wasn't giving an inch. "How did you come by the book?" he asked with all the authority of a circuit judge.

Devon turned slightly and, from the corner of his eye, he saw that Harry was steps away from the stone bench. He released the book immediately.

Phillipa dropped *The Rights of Woman* into the spacious pocket of the brown dress a moment before Harry would have been in a position to read the title.

"Why are you two fighting over a book?" he asked, looking pointedly at Phillipa's skirt pocket.

"We disagreed over a passage in *King Lear*," Devon said with calculated indifference and got up from the bench. "Have the horses been saddled for our ride?"

"Yes," Harry said. He clicked his tongue in reproval. "Your hat is askew, Phillipa."

"Don't you have some place to go, Harry?" she replied in a sulking display of temper.

He gave his sister a blistering look and turned back to his friend.

"I thought we would ride over to the Emerson estate. I would like you to meet Claudia's grandmother."

Devon laughed. "As good an excuse, as any, to set your eyes on the beauteous Claudia again."

"You would think I was a confirmed rake instead of

a gentleman, the way the old woman treats me," Harry lamented. "I would not even be going to London had the besom not made it clear that she wanted me to put some distance between Claudia and myself until the mourning period is over."

"I will charm Mrs. Emerson for you," Devon promised. "And you can pour sweet nothings into your beloved's ears outside the dragon's hearing." His lips rigid, he gave Phillipa a stiff, disdainful bow.

She watched the two men set off in lockstep for the stable. She owed Devon Roarke for not tattling to Harry. But she was not in a forgiving mood. He had no right to castigate her for reading *The Rights of Woman*. Men were incredibly condescending. They believed women were so weak-minded that they could not discern the dross from the gold in a controversial tract.

He had asked with utterly masculine assurance, "How did you come by the book?" as if he really expected an answer.

"It is not because my father has liberal notions about females, my lord," she said aloud. Her parent's inattention to financial matters had allowed her to purchase *The Rights of Woman*.

Phillipa presented Sir Nigel with the ledgers at the end of each quarter. Deploring the mundanity of keeping accounts, he would give the figures a cursory glance, utter the same, "Fine, fine, fine," and return to his horticultural journals.

Phillipa paid the bills, including the ones from the London bookseller from whom she ordered books for both her father and herself. Had Sir Nigel not allowed her free reign with the household expenditures, Mary Wollstonecraft's "depravations" would never have crossed Brookfield's threshold.

Cognizant that when Harry became master of the estate all that would change, Phillipa straightened her straw hat and the black shawl and got down to making necessary plans for her future.

Twenty minutes later she told Sir Nigel that she wished to go to London for the Season. From behind a library table covered with gardening books, he mulled over her request.

"Pip, I cannot afford to set up a house in Town," he said.

She sat beside a window where the sill was lined with red clay pots of various kinds of green herbs.

"Papa, I would not remove you from Brookfield and your gardens. I plan to go to Aunt Sally."

"Hmm." Sir Nigel stroked his strong chin and, finally, nodded in approval.

"Yes, I imagine, Sally would be delighted above the common to take you in hand. Lord Shaw is in Vienna with Lord Charing. She would welcome the diversion. Ladies do love dearly to arrange a Season."

"Whenever Aunt Sally writes, she always invites me to visit," Phillipa said to bolster her claim. Lady Shaw was a member of the *ton* and knew her way around the beau monde. "She will guide me in avoiding missteps. Under her wing, I shall learn how to go on in society."

Sir Nigel picked up an agricultural pamphlet that King George had written under a pseudonym; he put the booklet back down onto the desk without looking at it.

"I fear I have done you a great disservice, Pip. Your aunt pleaded with me to give you a Season the year after your mama died. I was still too bereaved at the time and refused to take proper note of her offer. Then, you and Lieutenant Baines met at the village assembly and seemed to come to an understanding. I should have sent you to London years ago."

"Do not rebuke yourself, Papa. I never thought of going before. I liked taking care of you. But I think it is time I looked for a husband."

Sir Nigel could not disagree. "Harry and Claudia will soon take over your duties. Right or wrong, it is the way things are. You may be the smarter, but your brother is the heir."

"Oh, Papa, you need not flatter me. I will go quietly. I know that there is no longer a place for me here." Her slender shoulders lifted in a resigned gesture.

Sir Nigel let his statement stand without further comment. He wished he could truly ease his daughter's hurt, but he would be doing her a bad turn if he did not resort to plain speaking.

"Spinsterhood has no pleasures, Pip. A woman's happiness lies in having a husband and a family of her own. I could stand between you and Harry for a time, but these old bones are not getting any younger. You would be miserable living here under your brother's thumb once I am gone."

"You shall live to be a hundred, Papa. But I am reconciled to finding a husband even at my advanced age of four and twenty, for plainly Harry and I cannot live peacefully under the same roof," she said, sounding for all the world as though she had been handed a prison sentence.

Sir Nigel smiled. "You know, Pip, you are not facing a Hobson's choice. Your mother and I had the happiest of unions. Marriage with the right partner can be exceedingly rewarding. Moreover, every man in the Marriage Mart is not seeking a seventeen- or eighteen-year-old bride. It just seems that way. Now, be a good girl and fetch me a cup of tea," he said, for despite his optimistic air, he felt tears begin to dim his eyes. He picked up the king's pamphlet and began to read the text with marked attention.

Thus dismissed, Phillipa went to do her father's bidding, but the spring in her step belied the sadness in her heart. She knew that by the end of the day when she was alone in her bed, she would become a veritable watering-pot. It was not easy to lose the position she had held since she was eighteen, nor to be pushed from the house where she had been born and had lived her entire life. But neither would she beat her breast and tear her hair in a useless battle against something that could not be changed.

Four

Phillipa had made up her mind that wedlock was to be her fate. Yet, she could not help but think that the world that Mary Wollstonecraft envisioned for her gender, where an intelligent woman could carve out a career for herself and live alone on her wages, was immensely more sensible than a loveless marriage. But in a male-dominated society such an option was not open to her. Female independence was tantamount to immorality and a sure road to social ruin in the collective minds of polite society.

Thus, Phillipa dutifully wrote to Lady Shaw and received a positive reply within days. Harry had to wait until Lord Darrington fulfilled his father's commission at Fairlea and sent word that he had removed to Town.

Phillipa and the viscount had not parted on the best of terms. Neither of them had given an inch. Lord Darrington's expression had remained haughty and Phillipa's frigid. The high-handed manner in which he had snatched *The Rights of Woman* from her pocket and scolded her as if she were a naughty child still galled her. He was, after all, no kinsman, a person who would have had some excuse for interfering in her life, but a near stranger, who had no say in her conduct.

Soon the anticipated summons came from the viscount and Phillipa and Harry bid Sir Nigel good-bye. They set off early one morning on the full day's trip to London in the family coach with a hired driver and James Newell up on the box beside the coachman.

Phillipa had been delightfully surprised when Harry had requested that James accompany him to London as his valet. But when she thanked her brother for giving the young man a chance, she had been unsettled by Harry's ungracious reply.

"Don't thank me," he had groused. "It is Devon Roarke's doing. He claims that James has the makings of a credible personal servant and egged me into putting him under Ransome's supervision." Although she was happy for James, she did not like being in debt to the viscount once again.

The long day's journey was proving to be boring for Phillipa, for the countryside beyond the coach window lacked scenic splendor. For periods, she and Harry chatted about this and that, for her brother's mood had improved to near cordiality since he had learned that Phillipa was in the market for a husband. But mostly Harry had lain back against the velvet cushions, his eyes closed on the borderland of sleep. Phillipa stared fixedly from the window, deep in her own thoughts.

When the coachman drove past the city limits, Harry stretched himself awake. Phillipa was amazed at the crowded thoroughfares and the sheer number of people in the streets. She remarked as much to Harry.

"The streets are crowded with vehicles in every part of town," he said, "but, at least, you do not have the lower classes cluttering the sidewalks in our part of London."

After some miles, the driver turned the horses into a tree-lined avenue. They stopped in front of an imposing town house which Harry identified to Phillipa as Lord Charing's London home.

Harry debarked; through the window, Phillipa saw James jump down onto the sidewalk. She had some latent misgivings about James being under Harry's care, for her brother had either ignored James during stops on the journey, or he had rudely ordered him around.

However, her concerns for the young valet-to-be fled her mind when Lord Darrington walked down the steps to the street and pumped Harry's hand. Phillipa kept her eyes on the viscount while the men talked; a footman helped James unpack Harry's luggage from the boot at the rear of the coach.

His Lordship was handsome and wore his elegant costly clothes well, she conceded. Phillipa noted his intricately tied cravat, as well as the creaseless blue frock coat and buff-colored pantaloons. But, alas, it was too bad he was such a bully.

She pulled back from the window when he left Harry's side, approached the coach, opened the door, and leaned in.

"Miss Westhaven, would you care to alight for a respite before continuing on your journey?" he asked, smiling politely.

Phillipa was unable to keep the frost from her voice when she replied, "Thank you, no. Lady Shaw's house is not much farther, I believe."

"As you wish," he said. The genial smile faded and a coolness stole into his blue eyes. He withdrew and Harry took his place.

"You can continue on now, Pip," her brother said. "Give my love to Aunt Sally." The door shut and the coach lurched forward.

Phillipa's heart pounded oddly. It was so unlike her

to bear a grudge. She tried to sort out her offended feelings, but remained unsettled in her mind. When she arrived at Lady Shaw's town house, she promptly forgot Lord Darrington.

Phillipa's Aunt Sally, who admitted to fifty-odd years, but looked a decade younger, was round and rosy, her light brown hair showing not a single strand of gray.

"Madame Roubineaux is an absolute female Beau Brummel," her aunt was telling Phillipa as the two women sat together in comfortable chairs in Lady Shaw's private sitting room after dinner. "I have commissioned her to design and sew your clothes because, like the Beau, Madame sets fashion, not follows it."

Springing up from her chair, Lady Shaw twirled in a circle. "This is one of Madame's dresses," she said of the apple green crepe. "And you shall have every conceivable frock just as fine, Pip, for morning and afternoon and evening. For visiting, for walking, for driving, for dancing. Pelisses and spencers, too."

"Oh my," Phillipa said, a little breathless at her aunt's display of exuberance and overwhelmed by the promise of such an extensive new wardrobe.

However, Sir Nigel had prepared his daughter for this eventuality, and she was not entirely surprised. "Your aunt, I know, will want to underwrite your Season, Pip," her father had explained. "I see no reason to ruin her pleasure. She has a generous heart and no children of her own on whom to spend her unlimited wealth. Flinging her offer back into her face would be ungracious."

Seating herself once more after Phillipa had duly admired the dress, Lady Shaw went on with her plans for her niece's launch into society. "And your bonnets, footwear, reticules, and parasols, in addition to your underthings, will come from the premier shops in Bond Street."

That had been the beginning. In the ensuing days, Phillipa was measured, poked, pricked with pins, and swathed in expensive fabrics by shop assistants under Madame Roubineaux's expert eye. Before long, the purchases from the Bond Street establishments were being delivered daily to the house in Curzon Street. But eventually the numerous visits to the finest stores and the dressmaker tapered off.

The day before the initial shipment of gowns from Madame Roubineaux's was due to arrive, Phillipa sat in one of her old dresses, a dark brown heavy cotton, at Lady Shaw's "at home." She felt like an absolute ragtag in the midst of the elegantly attired company surrounding her.

She chatted with a Lord Mears, whose roaming eyes kept wandering to a fashionable young woman on the opposite side of the drawing room. Finally, he excused himself to go to the object of his interest. Lord Darrington, who had been conversing with Lady Shaw, took his place at Phillipa's side.

She had seen the viscount arrive earlier, and had reluctantly admired his beige coat, tan breeches, and canary yellow vest. He wore the black Hessians she recognized as the ones James had been polishing on the back steps at Brookfield.

Her intention to remain mannerly lasted only until the viscount said, "Lady Shaw has given me permission to walk with you in the park across the street, Miss Westhaven. Kindly fetch your bonnet and a wrap."

"Try inviting me, my lord, instead of ordering me."

Devon was taken aback. The chit had the audacity to teach him manners. But fighting with her was not why he had come to see her today. His was a mission of peace.

"*Please*, Miss Westhaven," he said emphasizing the civility while barely keeping the mockery from his voice. "It is important that I speak with you privately. Harry does not know I am here, but this concerns him."

Phillipa's mouth set into a stubborn line until she remembered that she had been longing to escape from this room, where she was a mudhen thrust into a muster of peacocks.

To Devon's relief, in a sudden about-face, she said, "I will get my pelisse and bonnet."

Less than five minutes later, Devon and Phillipa had stepped from the curb into a street that had to be crossed in order to reach the park. Without a by-your-leave, the viscount dragged Phillipa into the endless flow of carriages and carts and began to weave through the traffic. Phillipa found herself holding on to the viscount's gloved hand for dear life.

"Step lively," he bellowed when a curricle came within inches of running them down. Phillipa's heart was pumping out of control as the viscount pulled her onto the safety of the opposite curb in front of the park gates.

Breathing hard, she glared up at him. "You are mad, sir! We could have been killed."

"Nonsense," he retorted. "You are in the city now, ma'am. You will have to become adept at dodging the traffic."

She walked beside him through the iron gates into the greenery of the small park.

"I am not so birdwitted as to try that again," she muttered.

The viscount laughed. "It will come with practice," he said.

"Never! I have no desire to put myself in a position to be squished beneath a knuckleheaded coachman's carriage wheels. Were you not aware of the rude words that were being hurled at us?"

"Rude words? Sounded more like obscenities to me. Burned your ears, did they, Miss Westhaven? Though I don't see why it should bother you. Doesn't Wollstonecraft preach that women should receive the same treatment as men?"

Phillipa gave him a quelling stare in place of a good set-down, for, to her consternation, no snappy retort came to her. She settled for saying, "I shall never do that again."

He chuckled. "Just how do you expect to return to Lady Shaw's? Fly like a bird?"

"Uh," Phillipa moaned in frustration. "I forgot."

But she had lost the viscount's attention. He was staring straight ahead, his lips widening into a bright smile.

"Ah," he crooned. He hastened their pace until he came abreast of a fancy tilbury parked in the road. A dignified gentleman in his thirties was about to hand up into the vehicle a pretty young woman whom Phillipa knew would be considered the ideal of the *ton,* with her blond hair and blue eyes.

"Marilee," the viscount hailed the petite female, who appeared to be still in her teens. She was attired in a chic fur-trimmed dusty rose pelisse and matching fur hat.

She turned and rewarded the viscount with a radiant

smile of instant recognition. "Why, Devon Roarke, when did you return from the Continent?"

"Some weeks ago, my dear, but my father sent me to Fairlea to enact some business in his stead. However, I am back in Town now for the Season." He carried the small gloved fingers she offered him up to his lips.

"Is Harry with you?" she asked when the viscount released her hand.

"He is. In fact," he said, turning toward Phillipa, "Miss Westhaven here is Harry's sister. But I have sad news for you, Marilee. Our Harry is all but leg-shackled to a Miss Emerson."

"Handsome Harry betrothed? How very bad of him. Half the females in London will fall into a decline at the news." She giggled at her own small jest. "Where are my manners? You know my cousin Francis Kiernon, don't you, Devon?"

"Good to see you again, my lord," Devon said to Marilee's escort. He turned to Phillipa. "Miss Westhaven, Harry's admirer is the Honorable Marilee Kiernon, and this is her cousin, the Marquess of Petersford."

Proper responses to the introductions were made all around. Those out of the way, Miss Kiernon said, "I do hope Harry will be coordinating our activities. He is so good at organizing amusing diversions to go here and there."

"You can be sure of it, Marilee," Devon said. "He plans to have a last fling before he becomes a staid married man."

The marquess and Phillipa exchanged soft smiles common between strangers who are not acquainted with each other. He then addressed her quietly while Devon Roarke and Miss Kiernon chattered on.

"You do not reside in London, Miss Westhaven," he

said. It did not sound like a question. He was of average height, passably good-looking with thinning blond hair, and fine gray eyes that creased at the corners into a mesh of tiny wrinkles.

"No, my lord, I am here for the Season, stopping with Lady Shaw, my aunt. My first time in the city," she answered.

"First time?" he seemed more reflective than surprised. "No previous Seasons?"

Phillipa shook her head. "When younger, I had an understanding with a gentleman who was killed during a naval skirmish. Even before that, I kept house for my widowed father in the country and have been doing so ever since."

"Brookfield," he said. This time there was no doubt that it was not a question. Reacting to her quizzical look, he explained, "Harry has spoken of his country seat."

The marquess looked toward where Lord Darrington was helping Miss Kiernon into the tilbury. "It appears my cousin and Lord Darrington have ended their discourse." He bowed to Phillipa. "Your servant, ma'am," he said and joined his cousin on the box.

After a few commonplace exchanges, the Kiernons drove off, and Phillipa and the viscount walked back toward Lady Shaw's house.

"What is the private matter about which you wished to speak with me, my lord?" Phillipa asked when they were in sight of the park gates. The viscount had still not broached the subject for which he had ostensibly asked her to walk out with him.

Lord Darrington seemed at sea for a moment. "Private matter? Oh yes, that. Miss Westhaven, I sensed that you were rather starched up when you dropped off

Harry in Grosvenor Square the other day. Since you are his sister, you will be included in the activities to which Miss Kiernon just alluded. For us to be at odds in public would not do at all, for it would surely be noticed. For the sake of propriety, can I count on you to be civil to me during the times that we are thrown together?"

"I am always civil, my lord, but you had no right to rip up at me. What I read is really none of your concern," Phillipa said, feeling a real need to point out his transgressions.

"Good gracious, are you going to start again? I sought this meeting because I do not want Harry to know that we are at daggers drawn."

Phillipa whooped. "Daggers drawn? How dramatic!"

He threw up both hands. "Do you accept my apology or not?"

"I don't remember hearing one. All right, my lord, I shall be *comme il faut* . . . behave with the utmost propriety, that is, when in your company.

"I know what it means," he grumbled and began running the traffic gauntlet back the opposite way, causing Phillipa to wail several times, "This is utterly beyond common sense!"

Five

Phillipa posed before the cheval glass in a fashionable dress that had been delivered that morning. The pale green muslin was embroidered at the hem with a fern leaf design. The style was exquisite; the workmanship superb; the fit perfect. Yet she sighed in sheer exasperation.

Turning from the full-length mirror, she sat down at her bedroom vanity and frowned at her image in the smaller glass.

Lady Shaw watched from a boudoir chair, her heart-shaped lips pursed thoughtfully as Phillipa removed the combs from her thick hair and loosed the rebellious mass onto her shoulders.

"Aunt Sally, even in this striking gown, I am a complete frump because of these ungovernable tresses. Do you think I might look a little more the thing in one of those new short haircuts?"

"Exactly what I was thinking," Lady Shaw said. "You have the natural curl which should do well in that style. I will send for Monsieur André, who wields the most talented scissors in London, and see what he can do."

The renowned barber arrived that afternoon. By the time he left, Phillipa had been transformed to Lady

Shaw's satisfaction into a young woman who would show to advantage in the grandest of London's drawing rooms.

Phillipa, too, was quite pleased with her new look. Not only had her hair been altered into springy brown curls, but also her face had been recast into a more discernable oval. Her brown eyes seemed larger and brighter, while her nose and mouth just somehow looked better.

Lady Shaw and Phillipa spent some time talking about the change, while a maid swept up the piles of brown clippings from the parquet floor.

"You are in very good looks, my child," Lady Shaw said. "In fact, nearly beautiful."

Phillipa laughed. "Beautiful? Oh, Aunt Sally, What stuff! as Harry would say."

"I said *nearly*," the older woman declared with a touch of asperity. "You are pretty enough to aspire to form a highly eligible connection.

Phillipa sighed. "I know I look better."

"A good deal better," Her Ladyship said. "Pip, don't let your confidence dip. I am not turning the butter boat over you. You do look pretty."

A knock at the bedroom door brought an end to the debate and sent Phillipa to answer the summons in the occupied maid's place.

Lady Shaw's butler stood on the threshold. He handed her a calling card and said, "Lord Petersford to see you, Miss Westhaven."

Taken by surprise, Phillipa looked at her aunt as if seeking guidance.

Lady Shaw took the card from her niece and glanced briefly at the caller's name.

"Mapes, show His Lordship to the upstairs drawing

room. Miss Westhaven will see him directly." When the butler closed the door and went off to discharge his duty, Lady Shaw said, "You must receive Lord Petersford, dear. He is too important a person to ignore. But, Pip, how do you come to be acquainted with him?"

"Lord Darrington made him known to me when the viscount took me for a stroll in the small park across the street yesterday. The marquess was with his cousin, a Miss Kiernon, but he and I exchanged no more than a few words."

Lady Shaw's eyes gleamed. "You must have made a favorable impression for him to call so soon. Francis Kiernon is excellent *ton* with a good income and a beautiful estate in the country. He is a widower with a young daughter, and it is no secret that he is searching for a wife." She did not know what had possessed Petersford to call on Phillipa, but this was an opportunity not to be missed.

"Go on, now; don't keep His Lordship waiting," she urged. Phillipa herself was too curious to offer dissent, and moved quickly to the door.

When she entered the drawing room, Lord Petersford was standing at the window, looking down into the busy street below. He turned and an odd expression of unease seemed to cross his features. He lifted a jeweled quizzing-glass from his vest pocket and fixed it into his eye. "I am not a man given to blandishments, Miss Westhaven, but you look quite the kick of fashion today."

"Thank you, my lord," Phillipa said, a little uncertain, for his cool tone conflicted with his compliment.

"I would bet a coachwheel the haircut is the result of Monsieur André's oh so wondrous scissors, and the divine gown?" His voice rose a little, sounding almost sarcastic.

Phillipa found it difficult to put her finger on why his words appeared to be couched in a sneer. His facial expression was, after all, rather bland.

"Madame Roubineaux created it."

"She dressed my late wife." The comment made Phillipa uncomfortable, for it, like the rest of the strange exchange, sounded almost snide. Yet, she might have imagined his derisive tone, although she certainly had not imagined the lack of a smile.

The marquess returned the quizzing-glass to his vest pocket. Phillipa was certain she heard him sigh.

However, his gray eyes became slightly more friendly when he asked, "Would you care to take a turn in Hyde Park with me, ma'am? My tilbury is parked in Lady Shaw's drive in the hands of one of her grooms."

A ride in the park in an open carriage appealed to Phillipa; she promptly accepted his invitation and left to fetch her wraps.

While Phillipa donned her dark green spencer and her bonnet with the lighter green ribbons, Lady Shaw beamed, hardly able to believe Phillipa's good fortune.

"Francis Kiernon is a catch, Pip. He is not too old for you, just a few years on the right side of forty. Fair in looks. And a marquess to boot. You have stolen a march on everyone," she crowed. A legion of ambitious Mamas were pushing their daughters to set their caps for the wealthy lord. What a coup it would be if Phillipa cut out all those better-credentialed ladies.

Seeing her aunt's rapture, Phillipa wondered if she should mention Lord Petersford's unusual behavior. But she was not given to snap judgments, and so began to make excuses. His expression might have been simply dour, not mocking. There must be many perfectly un-exceptionable gentlemen who rarely smiled. The marquess deserved good marks for calling on her before he knew of her transformation. Didn't that mean that he had liked her for herself when he first met her? Phillipa decided this last point weighed heavily in the marquess's favor. She took her leave of Lady Shaw, deciding to keep her earlier discomposures to herself.

Hyde Park, where the fashionable rode to be seen, was crowded with both road and foot traffic. Lord Petersford drove the tilbury at a decorous pace and commented almost cheerily about the London social scene. He would share some tidbit with Phillipa about a titled gentleman or lady in a passing carriage. But mostly he spoke of his estate, his preference for the country, and his neighbors there.

Phillipa contributed some stories about Brookfield and her own love of the rural life. She was glad that she had accepted the marquess's invitation to go for a drive with him, for he was gracious, and she was now more at ease in his company.

"Isn't that Lord Darrington and Miss Kiernon?" Phillipa said when a sporty curricle and four came toward them; she got a good look at the tall-hatted driver and his pretty passenger.

Phillipa saw Devon Roarke gaze at her blankly before sudden recognition caused him a moment's distraction. The curricle careened onto the grass and just missed hitting an iron bench.

Lord Petersford pulled to the side of the road and stopped. He and Phillipa looked back in time to see the viscount correct his near-disastrous miscalculation and

We'd Like to Invite You to Subscribe to Zebra's Regency Romance Book Club and Give You a Gift of 4 Free Books as Your Introduction! (Worth $19.96!)

If you're a Regency lover, imagine the joy of getting 4 FREE Zebra Regency Romances and then the chance to have these lovely stories delivered to your home each month at the lowest price available! Well, that's our offer to you and here's how you benefit by becoming a Regency Romance subscriber:

- 4 FREE Introductory Regency Romances are delivered to your doorstep

- 4 BRAND NEW Regencies are then delivered each month (usually before they're available in bookstores)

- Subscribers save almost $4.00 every month

- Home delivery is always FREE

- You also receive a FREE monthly newsletter, which features author profiles, discounts, subscriber benefits, book previews and more

- No risks or obligations...in other words, you can cancel whenever you wish with no questions asked

Join the thousands of readers who enjoy the savings and convenience offered to Regency Romance subscribers. After your initial introductory shipment, you receive 4 brand-new Zebra Regency Romances each month to examine for 10 days. Then, if you decide to keep the books, you'll pay the preferred subscriber's price of just $4.00 per title. That's only $16.00 for all 4 books and there's never an extra charge for shipping and handling.

It's a no-lose proposition, so return the FREE BOOK CERTIFICATE today!

Say Yes to 4 Free Books!
Complete and return the order card to receive this
$19.96 value, ABSOLUTELY FREE!

If the certificate is missing below, write to:
Regency Romance Book Club
P.O. Box 5214, Clifton, New Jersey 07015-5214
or call TOLL-FREE 1-888-345-BOOK
Visit our website at www.kensingtonbooks.com.

FREE BOOK CERTIFICATE

YES! Please rush me 4 Zebra Regency Romances without cost or obligation. I understand that each month thereafter I will be able to preview 4 brand-new Regency Romances FREE for 10 days. Then, if I should decide to keep them, I will pay the money-saving preferred subscriber's price of just $16.00 for all 4...that's a savings of almost $4 off the publisher's price with no additional charge for shipping and handling. I may return any shipment within 10 days and owe nothing, and I may cancel this subscription at any time. My 4 FREE books will be mine to keep in any case.

Name _____

Address _____ Apt. _____

City _____ State _____ Zip _____

Telephone ( ) _____

Signature _____

(If under 18, parent or guardian must sign.)

RN051A

Terms and prices subject to change. Orders subject to acceptance by Regency Romance Book Club.
Offer valid in U.S. only.

drive the powerful chestnuts safely back onto the right-of-way.

Phillipa had a sudden picture of Devon Roarke looking absolutely dumbfounded, and laughed.

"I fail to share your amusement, madam," the marquess said sharply and set his horses in motion. "Both His Lordship and my cousin could have been seriously injured or even killed."

"That was unkind of me, my lord. But the boggled expression on Lord Darrington's face when he made out that it was I . . ."

The marquess made a sound that passed for a chuckle. "Devon Roarke is a crack whipster. He will be mortified to have made a cake of himself with such cow-handed driving in public. See what happens when you tempt fate and make yourself into an Incomparable, Miss Westhaven. You turn a perfectly sane gentleman into an addlepated corkbrain."

"I am hardly an Incomparable, my lord," Phillipa said, caustically, for she had heard again that subtle trace of condemnation.

Lord Petersford looked straight ahead over his horses' backs.

"Perhaps not. I trust that you have more substance to you, Miss Westhaven. Incomparables, you know, are usually heartless care-for-nothings."

Phillipa remained silent rather than comment on a type of woman she knew nothing about, and remained so for the rest of the ride. But when the marquess left her at Lady Shaw's door, he said all the right things which took the sting out of his former bitterness. In any case, Phillipa had never felt his censure was really directed toward her. He seemed to have something against beautiful women, she thought, as she went into the Curzon Street house.

"How did you enjoy your ride with Lord Petersford?" Lady Shaw asked, putting aside the tablecloth which she was embroidering.

Phillipa took a chair and said, "Pleasant. Hyde Park was lovely, springlike and bright after last night's rain."

The state of the weather was not what Lady Shaw had in mind when she asked the question; however, she did not want Pip to feel that she could not go out on her own without facing an inevitable cross-examination when she came back to the house. So she stifled the burning curiosity to hear what had conspired between her niece and the marquess.

"Harry was here earlier," she said and handed Phillipa a sheet of paper. "He left this itinerary for you. He is taking over your social life, it seems. And that is to the good, for you should be in the company of a younger crowd rather than being obliged to make do with my circle of friends. However, I will claim you, Pip, for the Duchess of Clendon's ball on Friday the twenty-eighth, for she is one of society's leading lights and I won't chance whether Harry will take you or not."

"My goodness . . . ," Phillipa said, reading Harry's schedule aloud, "the opera tomorrow night, a Venetian breakfast, a visit to see the paintings at the Royal Academy, a rout, a picnic in the country, Kensington Gardens . . . I never suspected that Harry was the arbiter of the social events for his set."

"His is an exceptional group. Not a fribble among the gentlemen; well, perhaps one or two, but the ladies are prettily behaved, at least, for the most part." She laughed a little at her absurdity.

Phillipa, too, smiled at her aunt's limited endorsement and tucked the folded paper into her green beaded reticule. She glanced at the ormolu clock on the mantel, stood up, and walked to the door. "I must change for dinner." Pausing with her hand on the brass knob, she said, "Aunt Sally, were you acquainted with Lord Petersford's wife?"

"Why, yes, I was. She was exquisitely lovely, the toast of the Season."

"I thought as much," Phillipa said.

Lady Shaw made a clucking sound. "Now, Pip, do not start making comparisons. Marsha Kiernon was also an unconscionable flirt. Even after she and Francis were married, she encouraged other men to whisper pretty things into her ear. She made her husband miserable. I think he is wiser now and shall look for more enduring qualities in a wife and not marry an empty-headed Incomparable again."

Phillipa took several steps back into the room.

"You mean, Lord Petersford will eschew beauty this time around and will choose a wife with his head, not with his heart?"

Lady Shaw sighed at the trace of melancholy in Phillipa's voice. Everyone wanted a love match.

"That is not a bad way to approach a marriage, you know," she said, "even more so for a female than for a male. Security can be more important than sentiment as long as the gentleman is kind and not abusive."

"Yes, I suppose one must be practical. For my own peace of mind, as well as Harry's, it is incumbent on me to find a husband."

"But you need not rush into an ill-advised union to

satisfy your brother. You can come and live with me. Your uncle is gone nine months out of ten on the king's business. I would welcome your company."

Phillipa had to laugh. "I may take you up on your offer, Auntie, and, then, you will be sorry."

This drew a smile from Lady Shaw. "Believe me, Pip, I am too selfish by nature to burden myself with an unwanted relative. You are like a daughter to me."

She picked up her embroidery and set a stitch as Phillipa reached the door. "You may or may not want Petersford in the end, Pip," Lady Shaw said from across the room. "But he saw something in you he liked. Mark my words, he will be taking many more looks, a second, third, and fourth, before he makes up his mind."

Six

Lady Shaw proved quite prophetic. Lord Petersford did become particular in his attentions to Phillipa, although not to the exclusion of the other young women who frequented Harry's entertainments. Thanks to Harry, Phillipa was getting a well-rounded introduction to the London social scene. She would often exchange pleasantries with her brother's male guests and had made friends with several young women, although all were at least a half a decade her junior.

Harry had complimented her for acquiring a veneer of town bronze so rapidly. Now and then, she saw him speaking with Lord Petersford and glancing at her, causing Phillipa to wonder if she was a part of their conversation.

With a wicked gleam in his animated blue eyes, Lord Darrington had remarked to Harry in her hearing that females who insisted upon changing themselves into raving beauties from one day to the next should be required to post a notice in the park to warn unsuspecting drivers.

Phillipa's moment of reflective humor concerning the viscount waned as she made herself comfortable at Lord Shaw's desk in the library. She prepared to write to Sir Nigel about the whirlwind of activities she had been swept into since she arrived in London. For all his charm, Devon Roarke, for some reason, continued to rub her the wrong way.

At the opera, instead of listening attentively to Mozart's radiantly beautiful music, he had flirted outrageously with Marilee Kiernon from a seat directly in front of where Phillipa sat beside Lord Petersford. Miss Kiernon's continual tinkles of laughter provoked by the viscount's behavior had caused annoying interruptions to Phillipa's concentration.

Phillipa sharpened a quill and dipped the point into a pot of black ink. Of course, she would not write to her father about the viscount's serious want of conduct. She would instead tell him something of Lord Petersford, who was proving to be a chivalrous gentleman. Whatever had bothered him at first about her seemed to have been put to rest.

She wrote to her father that the marquess had gone over the German libretto of the night's opera *Die Zauberflöte* for her, since Phillipa did not speak the language.

"In English the title translates to *The Magic Flute,* a rather inane little fairy tale, but Mozart's fantastic music is well worth sitting through the torture of the mediocre story," Lord Petersford had said. His illuminating remarks were far more interesting a topic to relate in a letter than a lurid description of the monstrous liberties Lord Darrington took in public with a young woman of the *ton.*

Phillipa tapped the top of the pen against her teeth while she dispelled the viscount's unpleasant image and collected her thoughts about Harry's Venetian breakfast.

Papa, it was not a breakfast at all, but an afternoon feast held outdoors on the lawns of an estate Harry borrowed from an acquaintance who was absent from Town, she wrote.

Tables had been set with soft linen napkins and Honiton lace tablecloths, Willow Pattern china, and the best Sheffield silver brought over from Lord Charing's town house.

She added these details to the letter, but not that Francis Kiernon was actively seeking a wife and a stepmother for his small daughter.

Several matrimonial-minded young women had put themselves in the marquess's way. Gallantly, he had walked the flower-edged paths and green lawns with the would-be marchionesses. Yet, after he had filled a luncheon plate with creamed chicken in a flaky pastry, pickled mushrooms, and herbed rice for a notable Incomparable, he had quickly detached himself from the beauty. He had led Phillipa to a belvedere set on a hill which overlooked a small lake and challenged her to a game of dominoes. The tiles had been set out on the wooden table beneath the domed roof for the guests' convenience. She had often played on a winter's night with Sir Nigel and knew the game.

"Dominoes was introduced into England by French prisoners only about twenty-five or thirty years ago," the marquess had informed her. But, although Phillipa thought her father might find this interesting, she left it out of her letter. She did not want to invoke Lord Petersford's name repeatedly, or Sir Nigel might think she was actively setting her cap for the marquess.

The afternoon almost ended in disaster, she concluded her remarks about the Venetian breakfast after describing the food, a safe topic, *when the wind whipped up and a dark cloud came out of nowhere and dumped large drops of rain onto us. The servants dashed here*

*and there snatching up dishes and silver, tableclothes
and napkins. The gallant gentlemen herded us ladies to
the safety of the carriages. Although the storm passed
rapidly, the damage was done. Poor Harry's splendid
breakfast ended prematurely.*

Phillipa put down her pen and rubbed her middle finger where she had tightly gripped the instrument. What
should she write about the visit to the Royal Academy
of Arts?

Sir Nigel was familiar with the museum. In fact, her
father was the one who had said that the exhibits were
not to be missed.

"Your mother never tired of going there and viewing
the magnificent paintings," he had said.

Finally, Phillipa decided on a few lines to the effect
that the Academy was everything that Sir Nigel had
promised. She closed the letter with affectionate
daughterly sentiments, sanded the ink, and applied the
sealing wax.

Leaning back in her chair, Phillipa gave herself over
to remembering her encounter that day with Devon
Roarke.

She had wanted to view the paintings in silence, but
Lord Petersford enjoyed analyzing each work of art for
her. Good manners kept her from asking him to be
quiet, so when Harry and Miss Kiernon joined them
and began a conversation with the marquess, Phillipa
seized the opportunity to slip from her escort's side.

Rounding a corner, she came across Lord Darrington,
his arms crossed over his broad chest. He was totally
absorbed in a charcoal sketch of a street fiddler with a
performing monkey on a leash, which was one of a set
of four. She knew nothing of technique or perspective
or light and shadow, but found the stocking-weaver at

his frame and the blacksmith at his anvil wonderful slices of the daily lives of the working class.

"These drawings are truly remarkable, my lord," she said, pointing to the fourth picture, which was of a barmaid dispensing ale.

The viscount blinked and muttered, "Miss Westhaven."

Her intrusion seemed unwelcome to him, for he began to walk on until Phillipa said, "I wonder who did these. The sign says that the artist is anonymous."

Lord Darrington stopped and walked back to her side. "You think them remarkable, ma'am? The subjects are common folk. Modern society prefers lofty themes done in oil."

"Why would the Academy exhibit the drawings here in this great hall if they are unworthy of hanging in public as you imply?"

"Anyone, from the lowliest school instructor to England's highest-paid portrait painter, can submit his work. Someone who has influence with one of the board members must have talked him into giving the sketches a place in this inconspicuous corner."

Phillipa's face lit up. "I know why the drawings are anonymous. The artist is a woman!"

"Ridiculous!" the viscount snapped. "Whatever gave you such a cork-brained notion?"

"Simple deduction, my lord. Creative females are forced to conceal their identities behind the appellation, 'anonymous' or take on a male pseudonym to be taken seriously."

The viscount snorted. "The Academy does not consider the work of females for exhibition."

"Narrow male minds," Phillipa muttered with an unladylike sniff.

Without another word, the viscount had given her a silken smile and turned his attention to Miss Kiernon and Lord Petersford, who were approaching. Devon Roarke had gone off with Marilee, and Phillipa, once again, had found herself on the marquess's arm.

The chiming of the clock in the hall prodded Phillipa from her reverie. Devon Roarke did not like her very much, she thought, as she picked up the letter to Sir Nigel which would be added to Lady Shaw's mail for franking before being posted. Naturally she wanted to be liked, but if the viscount chose to remain distant and cool, it would not cause her any pang of regret. Even before the thought was fully formed, she knew that what she was thinking was a lie to save her pride.

Seven

Phillipa shook her head in disbelief and raised her normally well-modulated voice to be heard above the incessant chatter and untrammeled laughter that came at her from all sides.

"I see no earthly purpose to a rout, except as a ridiculous exercise in cramming as many people as humanly possible into a small space in a private residence," she said.

Mere inches separated Phillipa from Lord Petersford in a public room in Lord Charing's town house, where they were surrounded by a noisy mob of fashionably dressed ladies and gentlemen.

"I had quite forgotten what a mad crush these things are," the marquess agreed, sounding roiled. "I would offer to brave this rude horde and look for some champagne, Miss Westhaven, but I fear I would never find you again."

Before Phillipa could suggest that they might attempt to reach the champagne together, an insistent male voice hailed the marquess by his given name.

"Francis! Francis! Over here, man!"

Lord Petersford turned instinctively. He recognized the speaker and automatically stepped toward him, inadvertently cutting himself off from Phillipa. She tried to follow him, but a man here, a woman there, came between them until she could not catch sight of his blond head even when she stood on her toes and craned her neck. Having had quite enough of being elbowed and pushed, Phillipa waded through Harry's guests. She wormed her way to the perimeter of the room, where she leaned against the silver-papered wall. She closed her eyes to shut out the lunacy, only to jump when Lord Darrington spoke directly into her ear. "What a crush!"

"You gave me such a start, my lord!" Phillipa cried. With a trembling hand, she stilled the rapid rise and fall of her bosom beneath the delicate lace that edged the low neckline of her amber crepe gown.

"Sorry," the viscount said, in an off-hand unapologetic tone.

"This is ludicrous," he grumbled after several moments. "Come on." He snatched up Phillipa's hand and pulled her after him, working his way along the edge of the floor.

He stopped at a door, opened it, and drew Phillipa into a small room where moonlight came through an undraped window. He gave the oak panel a backward shove and closed them in.

The viscount struck the flint which he had taken up from beside a table lamp and lit the wick. With a huge sigh, he tumbled his athletic body into a comfortable chair of rich brown leather.

"Harry should be happy. Such an intolerable press of people has assured that his rout is a resounding success."

In the added light, Phillipa looked around the room that was now revealed to her as an artist's studio. An easel sat close to the window; well-stocked shelves held drawing paper, sketch pads, and books. Tall cups were filled with a variety of thick-leaded drawing pencils. On a bottom shelf were a number of open boxes containing charcoal sticks of varying lengths and widths.

"Are you the artist, my lord?" Phillipa asked, leaning against a handsome old desk.

"I don't paint, but sketching is an avocation of mine," was the viscount's indirect reply.

Phillipa noticed a large sketch pad on top of the desk. "May I look?" she asked. He made a small gesture with his hand, indicating assent.

Phillipa carried the pad to the table lamp and, in the better light, looked at a charcoal sketch on the inside page that was of a workman laying bricks.

Lord Darrington was very good. The picture in shades of black and gray, in her opinion, was the work of an artist with real talent. She looked at him, and although he was watching her, his expression gave away nothing of his thoughts.

Phillipa paged through the entire collection, before replacing the pad on the desk. "Impressive, my lord," she said, her hands clasped in front of her.

"Thank you," he replied.

"You could easily be a professional illustrator," she claimed, wondering in which book she had seen similar drawings just recently.

"Don't do it up too brown, Miss Westhaven," he said with a small, dry smile.

Phillipa's bright eyes rounded in a sudden epiphany as the obvious occurred to her. It had not been in a book that she had seen the drawings. "The charcoal sketches at the Academy are yours, my lord," she said with awe.

The muscles twitched in his lean cheek, bearing witness that her shot had hit the mark. "I would be obliged, ma'am, if you did not make that observation in the presence of others."

"If you are intent on hiding your light under a bushel, why did you submit your drawings for possible exhibition?"

"Now therein lies a tale," he said, drolly. "During a bout of immoderate drinking, Harry decided that I should exhibit my work at the Academy. I concurred as long as I could remain anonymous. The idea which seemed brilliant the previous night, struck me as corkbrained in the morning. But, alas, I neglected to make my change of heart known to Harry, and he did not ask."

Phillipa smiled. "I can see what's coming."

"Yes, I imagine you can. Harry pilfered the charcoals and submitted them. He found it vastly amusing when the drawings were accepted and hung."

"But why won't you claim ownership now that your talent is validated?"

"I see no point, Miss Westhaven. Artists exhibit in order to bring attention to themselves in hopes of generating sales or attracting patrons. What need have I of either? Sketching is just a hobby."

Phillipa could not argue with his reasoning. She picked up a smaller pad from the desk and opened the cover. Her face brightened. "You have captured my brother with amazing accuracy," she said. "And Papa, too," she cried when she looked at the next sketch of Sir Nigel. She turned the page and sucked in her breath.

The drawing was of her. She sat on the stone bench in the chapel garden, her old black shawl around her shoulders. Her difficult-to-manage hair escaped in untidy tendrils from beneath the brim of her ancient straw hat. Her expression was doggedly stormy as she clutched a book to her breast.

"How could you?" she wailed.

Devon raised a brow. "Let me see," he said. He eyed the drawing she held up. Damn! He had forgotten about sketching her after their encounter in the garden. In truth, the drawing was a fair rendering of her appearance that day. However, he knew he was being brazen and insensitive when he asked, "What bothers you?"

What bothered Phillipa was that the viscount had seen her as a complete drab. The veriest dowd. Her vanity was seriously bruised. While she had been admiring his good looks at Brookfield, he had been repulsed by her homeliness.

Phillipa had worked herself into a temper. She lifted her chin in open defiance. "Why include the book clapped to my bosom? Is that some sort of symbol that intelligent women are ugly, or is it that men admire beauty and find no value in a female with an inquiring mind?"

He shrugged. "Can't say, my dear, that I know a single fellow who finds a woman's mind wildly attractive."

Phillipa fumed. "Having good looks is all that counts when a man seeks a bride. Is that it?"

He remained maddeningly calm.

"Not entirely," he drawled. "But that is not solely a male matter. Every woman cannot be a diamond of the first water. Yet females deliberately try to be, enhancing their appearance to lure a man into marriage. You are my proof, Miss Westhaven."

"I?" Phillipa squealed.

The viscount rose languidly from the comfort of his chair and placed his hands on Phillipa's shoulders. Turning her to the wall, he forced her to confront her image in a mirror.

"Compare your reflection in the glass with the drawing in my sketch pad, and swear to me that you have made no changes in your appearance to attract a husband."

Phillipa was rendered speechless. He had her dead to rights.

Suddenly his hands were warm on her bare shoulders. She became very conscious of his touch; she turned from the mirror to cause him to drop his hands, which he did, but now he faced her and stood way too close. Her heart began to beat rapidly, for he cupped her cheeks with both hands and stared into her face as if he were memorizing her features. She gazed back at him in a cloud of confusion, unable to move.

Devon traced the contours of her cheekbones with his long fingers and wondered how he had missed seeing that she actually had a rather wonderful face. Although it was not in a mode which one would normally associate with beauty, for her nose and mouth might be considered unimpressive, she was far from plain. He must have been blind not to have noticed her rich brown eyes, splendid cheekbones, and creamy skin.

"I must re-draw you, my dear," he said softly. "You are bang up to the mark these days and look nothing like the portrait in my sketch pad."

The warmth of his voice was a caress. Phillipa was afraid she would collapse away in a dead faint, for his smile was not disdainful or indifferent, but paradise to behold.

But, too soon, his hands left her face, and he went to douse the light. He opened the door and bowed her out into the main room. Phillipa felt absurdly happy. Devon Roarke did like her, after all.

Most of Harry's guests had gone home or on to other entertainments. Phillipa and Lord Darrington sailed across the thinned-out floor to where Harry was sipping champagne from a long-stemmed glass as he talked with Marilee Kiernon.

When Phillipa and Devon joined them, Marilee whispered something to Devon from behind her fan. He laughed. "You will excuse us," he said to Harry and Phillipa, and the two walked off arm in arm.

Phillipa watched them. She had always considered herself a woman who used her head. Yet she had gone into an emotional dither when Devon Roarke had been warm and gentle to her. She had put too much significance into a simple act of kindness. Not being a cruel man, the viscount had perceived her hurt and had atoned for causing her pain by promising to draw a more flattering portrait of her.

Why this should have caused such an upheaval of emotions inside her, she could not even guess. Perhaps it was because the viscount had never been so nice to her before. But she put aside her contemplation when Lord Petersford came to stand beside Harry and her.

After a short, polite exchange between the two men, Harry turned his attention to a departing guest.

Lord Petersford said to Phillipa, "I tried to reconnect with you after our separation, but I could not find you in the earlier mob scene. The buffet seems to be accessible at last. Shall we?"

"Indeed, my lord," Phillipa said amiably and linked her arm through his, content to be led to the food.

Eight

Phillipa sat alone beneath a willow tree on the banks of a stream, tossing pebbles overhand one at a time into the clear water. Nearby, in the green meadow of the quiet countryside where Harry had transported his guests by carriages from London, servants were collecting scattered dishes and silverware and repacking leftovers from the *al fresco* meal into picnic hampers.

Under the trees, young women in flowered gypsy hats and pastel muslin frocks gossiped and laughed together. Here and there a sleepy male guest napped in the shade, while couples strolled arm in arm beside the brook.

Devon had his shoulder propped against the trunk of an oak tree while he conversed with Lord Mears, a young aristocrat, several years his junior. His eyes kept darting in Phillipa's direction. Finally, giving into an impulse, he left the duke's side and walked over to Phillipa. He dropped down on the grass beside her and draped his long arms over his raised knees.

She gave him a welcoming smile which he returned in full measure.

"It seems, Miss Westhaven, we have been abandoned by Lord Petersford and Miss Kiernon. They walked off together some time ago, and I haven't seen them since." He winked at her conspiratorially. "But, fortunately, our romantic interests are quite safe since Marilee and Francis are first cousins."

Phillipa looked askance. "You are mistaken, my lord, to link the marquess and me romantically."

He chuckled engagingly. "Semantics, Miss Westhaven, but linked you are. Francis is looking for a wife, and I would bet a pony that you are first in the running."

"I am very certain that I do not make Lord Petersford's heart bump," she said, smoothing the skirt of her blue muslin frock.

"Lord help me. Surely you are not expecting to fall in love the way your brother has." The viscount cocked a thumb in the direction where Harry sat with his back against a large rock. Across his knees was a lap desk. "Even here at a picnic, he is writing a letter to Claudia."

"No, I am not looking for a love match," she said honestly. "Still, it must be wonderful to be approaching marriage as Harry is with someone he truly loves, instead of simply making an accommodation."

"Don't overestimate the merits of love. Brains can be a more reliable means to a successful marriage than mindless ardor. Romantic or not, Francis Kiernon is a splendid catch. He would make you an excellent husband." Their eyes locked for a serious moment.

But the viscount's impish grin broke the somber mood. "You know, Miss Westhaven, the marquess has a high sense of honor and will probably not beat you, even if he finds you reading seditious books."

Phillipa wrinkled her nose at him. "What a relief," she said, wryly. "But, it is a moot point, sir, since Lord Petersford has not offered for me in form or otherwise. What of you and Miss Kiernon? Is there to be a match?"

Lord Darrington did not answer at once. He picked up an imbedded pebble from the grass and lobbed it across the stream, sending a cluster of gnats rising from the tall weeds on the opposite bank,

"My father tells me I need a wife," he said. "No doubt, Marilee would make a dutiful one who would defer to me in all things. She knows the rules and would play by them. If our marriage proved dull and I stopped dancing attendance on her and went my own way, she would not go into a decline, but would find balm in her own pursuits."

"But she could not find the same sort of amorous solace elsewhere as you would," Phillipa pointed out. "You would expect her to remain faithful to you."

The viscount rolled his eyes skyward. "Am I to be regaled with more of Mary Wollstonecraft's rebellious tenets? Is there no end to your admiration of the woman?"

"There is much to be said for what's good for the gander is good for the goose. Why is it that once a woman forfeits her virtue she can never regain her respectability? It is lost forever, while a gentleman preserves his no matter how often he indulges in vices."

"You know, Miss Westhaven, you are confusing freedom with irresponsibility."

"Irresponsibility? It is harum-scarum males who populate the country with their by-blows."

His expression became harsh and unsmiling. "As I said, ma'am, Miss Kiernon knows the rules and would abide by them. And let's not forget that Madam Mary died with her reputation in shreds. Is that what you strive for?"

"While Mary Wollstonecraft did make a shambles of her life with poor choices, it does not mean that some of her ideas are not valid or that women, in general, lack intelligence and should be treated as mindless inferior beings," Phillipa said with a dogged persistence. "Yet, I fear that I am not strong enough to go against convention. I have no intention of modeling my life on hers."

"I should hope not," His Lordship said. He stretched out his long legs and leaned back onto his elbows. "Let's call a truce, ma'am. I am weary of our hollow bickering. The day is too fine for wrangling."

Phillipa nodded her concurrence.

For a time there were only the sounds of their immediate world. Insects buzzed, the brook gurgled, and small birds sang in the willow branches. The day was alive with the chirping of crickets while indistinct human voices drifted from the near distance.

"How is James Newell progressing under Mr. Ransome's tutoring?" Phillipa asked after several moments of a silence that was oddly companionable.

"Remarkably well. In fact, Ransome is quite proud that your protégé learns so quickly."

They went on in an amiable manner, discussing the young man who had been brought to London against Harry's wishes to study to be a valet.

"Why did you intercede with Harry in James's behalf?" Phillipa asked. "I have always wondered."

"Why did you care whether Newell got a chance to be a valet or not?" he countered.

She gave her shoulders a small shrug. "Too many servants are treated as if they are less than human and have their feelings trampled upon. James has a right to pursue his dream."

Devon looked into her face and wondered again why he had ever thought she looked ordinary, when she had such speaking brown eyes. He even admired her proud bearing and the determined set of her head when she defended her wrong-headed ideas.

"I don't often disagree with Harry," he said, "but I did not like by half his treatment of the lad. Showing personal animosity toward a servant who cannot fight back is small-minded. I put Harry straight, but it earned me nothing but one of his famous black scowls."

Phillipa reveled in the moment of like-mindedness between them. But her enjoyment of finding a point of complete accord with Lord Darrington on an important matter was short-lived.

Lord Petersford had been searching for Phillipa; when he saw her sitting on the bank of the creek with Devon Roarke, he walked over and reached out his hand to her.

Making his apologies to the viscount, he said, "Come, Miss Westhaven. I have spotted a nest of baby geese. You must see them."

Phillipa permitted the marquess to help her up, although, for just a moment, she wished he had stayed away and that she could have continued her pleasant tête-à-tête with Lord Darrington.

The mother goose flapped her wings and ran menacingly at Phillipa and the marquess when the intruders approached her nest. Laughing at the hostile bird's aggressiveness, the humans retreated to a safe distance.

"I fear, ma'am, I have not been exactly candid with you," Lord Petersford said when the combative mother returned to her downy-feathered children. "My true purpose was not to show you the recently hatched goslings, but to draw you off from prying eyes to a place with some privacy."

Phillipa's heart skipped two beats. She suspected what was coming, but she was not at all sure that she wanted to hear his declaration. But the choice was not hers.

He scratched his chin thoughtfully. "As you know, I have been a widower for two years and made no secret of the fact that I came to London to seek a wife and stepmother for my small daughter. Your brother has praised your ability to run a country establishment, which weighs heavily with me, for I have no great love for town life and much prefer to live at my country estate. I think you get my drift, dear lady, as to where I am going with this spadework; may I go on?"

His cool gray eyes held nothing of a lover's warmth, but Phillipa said, "Yes, my lord."

"I find your maturity and even disposition much in your favor," he said, smoothly sincere. "Our many opportunities for private conversation have convinced me that we are compatible and shall deal well together."

Francis Kiernon had had an inkling from the first moment he had set eyes on Miss Westhaven that she would be the one he wanted for his wife. Plain though she was, there had been something in her bearing and quiet, assured manner which had appealed to him. He'd had a bad moment when Lady Shaw had overnight transformed her into a duplicate of the fashionable type of chit he deplored. The last thing he needed was a woman who attracted and encouraged the wrong sort of man, and shamed him with her wanton conduct as Marsha had done.

But Miss Westhaven, fortunately, had proved to have exceptionally good sense and had a grip on the kinds of impropriety which would raise eyebrows. And while she did look different now on the outside, which in retrospect was to her credit, he was certain that inside she was the same woman to whom he had been drawn that first day in the park.

Phillipa found herself wishing that the marquess would say that he loved her and kiss her senseless. But she put aside such mooncalf whimsies. She had never expected Francis Kiernon to tender a romantic proposal, so she had no reason to feel cheated.

Lord Petersford's chiseled features gentled. "If you will consent to marry me, my dear, I shall do my best to be a good husband."

Phillipa knew she should say something, but her usually adroit tongue deserted her. The marquess sensed her hesitation, for he bridged the gap. "Take a few days to ponder my proposal. I do not expect a yea or nay today on such a serious step. After all, once the vows are said, there will be no going back."

He took her arm and tucked it beneath his to take her back to the picnic. He had been kind and gentle while making his less-than-romantic proposal. As was expected of her, Phillipa thanked him for the honor he had bestowed on her by asking her to be his wife; she promised to give his offer the careful consideration it deserved.

Phillipa's mind was at sixes and sevens that evening. She had little patience to expend on small talk with her aunt; she went to bed early, not to sleep, but to engage in a verbal jousting match with herself on the pros and cons of becoming Lord Petersford's marchioness. His warning made her realize that she must be very sure before she accepted him. *Once the vows are said, there will be no going back.*

She had heard enough about the marquess from others to know that he would be a constant husband and not seek entertainment elsewhere. He did not care about social prominence and would keep close to home. It was difficult to say precisely what was holding her back. She did feel a little guilty because he did not know her mind as well as he thought he did. He had guided the direction of their conversations and prescribed the subjects. She had never talked freely with him as she had with Devon Roarke, for instance. Yet Lord Petersford could be her last chance to make an auspicious match and avoid the dreaded fate of spinsterhood.

She had still not come to a firm resolution the next afternoon as she strolled beside Lord Petersford along the winding, shaded paths of Kensington Gardens. In truth, she was leaning toward accepting the marquess despite the fact that even today his attitude was hardly loverlike. But she had never expected to make a love match, but only a marriage of convenience that had reasonable expectations for a contented life. A union with him promised such a future. Married to Francis Kiernon, she would never ascend to the heights of ecstasy, but neither would she descend into an abyss of heartache.

"I believe there is some sort of entertainment going on where those men and women have gathered," he said, pointing to a group of people standing in a circle at the side of the walkway. "Let us see what is going on."

He hurried her to the edge of the small crowd. There they joined in the laughing and clapping for three tiny brown-and-white performing dogs that were jumping through a hoop at the direction of a small, mustached man who called the commands in French. While the animals danced on their hind legs and somersaulted in the air, Phillipa applauded, but her mind wandered back to the marquess's proposal.

She would be a fool to snap her fingers at a highly advantageous match that would tie her to a fine gentleman; it would make her the titled mistress of a beautiful home on one of the richest estates in the county.

The performance ended, and Harry joined her and Lord Petersford as the spectators dispersed. The Frenchman left with the three dogs at his heels and a hat full of coins in his hand.

"I reserved a table where we can take refreshments," Harry said. "Where are Devon and Marilee?"

"There they are." The marquess inclined his head toward where the couple were walking a short distance down the footpath from them. "I'll fetch them," he volunteered and set off.

Harry took Phillipa's arm and led her to the dining terrace.

"Francis seems quite taken with you, Pip. Dare I ask if he has made a move?" he said as he pulled out a straight-backed chair for her and seated himself in one on the opposite side of the table.

"His Lordship has proposed," Phillipa admitted, and perhaps because the benefits of being the marquess's wife were fresh in her mind, she said, "I think I shall have him."

Harry let out a whoop. "Splendid, Pip. I put in a good word for you, you know."

"Sh, Harry," she shushed him, aware of the approach of the marquess, Marilee, and Lord Darrington.

"It would not do for you to say anything before I have given Lord Petersford my answer."

"Mum's the word," her brother whispered, twisting his fingers before his lips, simulating the turn of a key in a lock.

While awaiting service, Marilee said, unhappily, "I am devastated since I will not be able to attend the Duchess of Clendon's ball."

"What happened?" Phillipa asked. "You were describing the gown you had made especially for the affair to me only yesterday."

"My grandmother is coming for an unexpected visit," Marilee said.

The waiter appeared and Harry gave him the order.

"Can you not excuse yourself for the one night?" Phillipa said.

Lord Petersford, who sat beside Phillipa, put his gloved hand on the sleeve of her blue woolen spencer.

"Our grandmother is the matriarch of the family and demands Marilee's attendance. My cousin's dowry depends on the old lady's generosity. It would not do to step wrong with her."

"Oh," Phillipa said. "Have you been commanded to appear as well, my lord?"

He smiled. "No, my dear, I have my own income. But I am afraid I must return to my estate on business. That is why I, too, have sent the duchess my regrets."

Marilee pouted prettily and lowered her lashes. "Devon threatens not to go to the ball because I won't be there. Add your entreaties to mine, Miss Westhaven, and convince the odious man he must attend."

The conversation halted there when the waiter appeared with the pots of tea and scones. During the disbursement of the refreshments, only a word here and there relating to the business of serving was exchanged.

But as Phillipa took her first sip of tea, her eyes met Lord Darrington's over the rim of her cup. "Well," he challenged, "aren't you going to coax me, ma'am?"

Phillipa laughed and set her cup onto its matching saucer. "I doubt that my persuasive powers are sufficiently honed to prevail in such an endeavor, my lord."

He smiled slowly at her. "Oh, I don't know about that. Try." The warm look in his blue eyes sent a jolt of pleasure through Phillipa. Devon Roarke was flirting with her.

Before she could form the glib words on the tip of her tongue into a coherent sentence, Harry spoke up. "Ignore the clown, Pip," he said genially. "He is merely playing with you and Marilee. We both have already sent our acceptances to the duchess."

Nine

Phillipa had found it strange when Lord Mears gained Lady Shaw's permission to take her into the first set at the Duchess of Clendon's ball. The young duke had never shown any preference for her company during Harry's recreations. And, when he said, "Would you honor me by allowing me to partner you at supper?" she was clearly astonished, especially given his cool reserve.

Yet His Lordship had always comported himself well, so she had agreed, but a second later she rued her decision when he explained rather autocratically, "Petersford asked me to stand in for him, you know. As is customary, I shall, therefore, claim the waltz before supper, as well."

Annoyed by Lord Petersford's high-handed presumption in providing a proxy for himself, Phillipa almost reversed herself. But she could not take out her irritation on Lord Mears, who would be insulted if she changed her mind. It wasn't that important, in any case, with whom she took supper.

The pique brought on by Lord Petersford's meddling passed when she was asked to dance by a titled gentleman. He paid her a lavish compliment which was accompanied by a smile of great charm.

The night sped on, as Phillipa went from one partner to another, in dance after dance, and set after set. Fortified by the tributes showered on her by attentive swains, she took heart that Madame Roubineaux's creation, a rose-pink silk evening dress embellished with pearl rosettes at the low neckline, became her so well.

Late in the evening, while she was engaged in an amusing conversation with her latest partner, a Mr. Hawkins, during a break in the dancing, she noticed Devon Roarke. He looked quite handsome in expensively tailored black-and-white evening clothes, watching her from across the room. She smiled spontaneously in the viscount's direction and saw him at once make a beeline toward her across the dance floor.

Devon had drifted into the ballroom while taking a breather from playing cards with Harry and some of their friends. He had not meant to dance with Phillipa. He had not meant to dance at all. But, she was most enticing in a dark pink confection that shimmered when she moved. The lustrous silk clung provocatively to her white breasts and the gentle curves of her body. Like a lodestone, her smile drew him to her.

He greeted Mr. Hawkins by name and spoke a few words to the gentleman before he asked Phillipa to stand up with him for the upcoming reel. Mr. Hawkins took this as a sign that his presence was *de trop,* bowed to Miss Westhaven, and took off to find a partner of his own.

The corners of Devon's mouth lifted in a smile of open admiration. "You are as fine as fivepence this evening, ma'am. And you are having fun, too," he said. She laughed. The sunniness of it lit up the room.

"You might say that. The gentlemen of the *ton* are

such good dancers," she said, a lively sparkle lurking in the depths of her brown eyes.

The musicians had concluded their intermission and returned to the podium, a signal for Phillipa and Devon to take their places for the country reel. The music began and Devon proved that he did not have two left feet either. He executed each complicated step faultlessly to the very end of the spirited dance.

Breathless, Phillipa fanned her warm cheeks with her ivory fan. She held out her hand for the viscount to lead her back to Lady Shaw's side now that the dance was over. Her heart raced with delight when he said instead, "I haven't had such a workout in weeks. The duchess has a splendid garden. Let's take a cooling stroll."

He lifted two champagne flutes from a passing waiter's tray and handed a glass to Phillipa. She walked beside him to the French doors and outside into the soft night air. They went down the wide steps to where colored lanterns in the trees illuminated the brick walks close to the house.

Their conversation remained light and trivial as they stopped occasionally to admire the spring flowers and to sip their champagne. Phillipa was too enthralled with Lord Darrington's affability to note with any clarity that they had meandered farther and farther into the heart of the garden where the trees no longer glowed with lanterns. Only the light of the half-moon showed them the way. Neither did it occur to her that they had not passed another couple in some time and appeared to be quite alone in this darkest part of the yard.

The viscount took her hand and led her off the walk into a small clearing, screened by thick shrubbery. He handed her into one of a pair of wrought iron lawn chairs hidden there and sat down in the other.

"This is a good place to catch the night breezes and cool off," he said, setting his wineglass beside hers on the low table between them.

Breathing in the heady scent of honeysuckle, Phillipa thought the isolated hideaway seemed designed for couples who wished to attain some amorous privacy. She leaned back in her chair and smiled to herself. The viscount had detoured unerringly from the brick path to the well-concealed lawn furniture.

"You have been here before," she said, laughing.

He chuckled. "A few times."

"And, probably, shared a kiss with Miss Kiernon."

"Good Lord, no!" he protested, but he did not sound offended. "I would never be so foolhardy as to kiss Marilee. She has yet to see her nineteenth birthday. Chits that age can get wrong ideas before a man is ready to commit himself."

He ran an idle finger along the edge of the metal table. "Now, should I kiss you, Miss Westhaven," he said, his voice full of fun, "that would be an entirely different matter."

"How so, my lord?" Phillipa directed a flirtatious glance at him and played along.

"Have you not professed to be a worldly woman? Surely, as a disciple of Mary Wollstonecraft's, you would not take it amiss or too seriously if a man found you so attractive he could not resist capturing your lips with his own."

"You do me an injustice, sir," Phillipa said in a silvery voice. "I never meant that a gentleman should take advantage of a woman. And I am far from worldly, having lived all my life in the country. But sharing a kiss, if it is pleasurable for both parties, cannot be wrong, I think."

Devon drained his wine from the glass, set down the empty champagne flute on the table, and stood up. He reached out both hands to her.

"How could you judge if my kisses were pleasurable unless you auditioned me?" In the dim moonlight, Phillipa could just make out the devilish glint in his eyes.

Feeling wickedly mischievous herself and not thinking beyond the moment, Phillipa said, "I concede your point, my lord," stood up, and stepped into his extended arms.

Devon wound his hands around Phillipa's waist and pulled her close. She rested her hands on the curve of his broad shoulders and tilted her face up toward his. Her heart began to beat a little faster.

Devon lowered his head, placed his mouth onto hers, and caressed her lips in a sweet, languid kiss and stepped back.

"How was it?" he asked.

Phillipa breathed a sigh. "I have had better," she lied. The pressure of his mouth had shaken her to her toes as Cedric's carefully chaste kisses never had done.

Fibber. Devon smiled to himself. The lady had trembled in his arms when his lips had touched hers. She had felt the beginnings of the flare of heat as much as he had. *Had better, eh? We'll just see about that.*

"Give me another chance," he pleaded and spread his hands theatrically in supplication.

Without hesitation, Phillipa's arms went around Devon's neck. When he reclaimed her lips, his deepened kiss quickly blazed into a hot urgent melding of their mouths that was hungry and seeking.

Phillipa tilted her head back when Devon's lips moved

to her neck and ever lower to feather the tops of her breasts.

Mind-melting passion surged through her veins as she made inarticulate love sounds of pleasure. Devon brought his mouth back to her lips in another long, scorching kiss that might have gone on forever had he not heard low voices beyond the shelter of the shrubs.

He groaned and wrested his mouth from hers. He was not the only gentleman present tonight who knew about this hidden nest. They might be getting company.

Deprived suddenly of his lips, Phillipa popped open her eyes. Devon was looking over her head, his face hard with concern. Her heart went flat. Was he disgusted with her wanton behavior?

Devon relaxed when the voices faded into the distance. He looked down at Phillipa with a slowly dawning smile and rubbed the satin flesh of her cheek with the ball of his thumb.

"Upon my soul, Pip," he whispered. "It seems we have discovered a decided partiality for each other."

His tenderness eased Phillipa's fears and she leaned into him. He put his arms on her back and pulled her close.

Devon dared not kiss her again, but he could not yet let her go. Just another moment, he said to himself. He moved his hand in a soothing circle over her spine.

Phillipa was not used to an embrace where she could feel the thrum of a man's heart. But it felt so right. She had never had any thought of catching Devon Roarke, but now he was the only man in the universe for her.

Devon sighed and murmured, "You are breathtakingly lovely, my sweet, and I am disinclined to have you leave my arms, but the supper dance must be about to start. With whom are you promised?"

"Lord Mears," she replied, still too dazed to think clearly.

His hands on her shoulders, he stepped back and looked down at her. "Lady Shaw will be anxious if the duke goes to claim you, and you are not there." Only then did some sense of what was fitting behavior come through to Phillipa.

"Your absence might cause talk," he reminded her. "We had best return to the ballroom immediately." She nodded.

Devon slid a hand to the small of Phillipa's back and kept it there until they passed through the French doors into the candlelit ballroom where a waltz was in progress. He bent his head close to hers and pressed her hand. "We both need time, Pip, to sort out our feelings."

"It is all so unexpected, my lord." Phillipa lifted her shoulders in a lame gesture. Had Lord Petersford been here tonight, she would have gone into the garden with him, not Devon. She had planned to accept Francis Kiernon's offer of marriage, not even aware that she loved another man.

Devon smiled gently. "Don't look so downpin, sweetheart. Unexpected, yes, but not unfavorable or appalling. In fact, it strikes me as quite promising, don't you agree?"

Before she could respond, Lord Mears materialized at Phillipa's side, and she became the recipient of a pointedly eloquent stare.

"I have been searching for you high and low for some time, Miss Westhaven. The waltz is already half over." Without so much as an apology to Devon, the young duke whirled Phillipa into the press of dancers.

Devon watched her waltz with Mears for a few moments, decided that he needed more time to put what happened into perspective before making an irreversible move, and went off to meet Harry for supper.

Hours later he removed Marilee Kiernon's picture from the walnut frame he kept on the night table beside his bed. He replaced it with the drawing of Phillipa he had sketched the day after Harry's rout.

He awakened the morning after the ball to her face smiling at him from the picture frame on his bedside table. He smiled back at the drawing and pulled on the clothes his valet had laid out the previous night. He sat down in his favorite wing chair and sipped coffee from an earthenware mug a servant had brought to his bed chamber a few minutes earlier.

Last night he had realized that his fondness for Marilee was more akin to an older brother for a younger sister than a true man-woman relationship. He could not imagine kissing Marilee except on the cheek or brow; the kisses he had shared with Pip had stirred a wild excitement in him such as he had never remembered experiencing before and which he even this moment longed to repeat.

He was no novice in lovemaking. And it was just possible that the attraction between them could be lust not love, but he did not think so. What he felt for Phillipa was too strong and had elements of need and tenderness as well as a powerful passion. It was different from anything he had felt before while making love to a woman. Heaven only knows what would have happened in the duchess's garden if the passersby had not brought him to his senses.

Devon rolled a mouth full of the strong black coffee around on his tongue. He was definitely thinking marriage. True, to him a suitable mate was a wife who would obey the laws he laid down. Such a favorable prospect was not likely to come about with Pip, who had this ridiculous notion that men and women were equal in all things.

But he had been over this sticking point again and again last night. He knew then, and he knew now, that he could draw up a long list of reasons why he and Phillipa did not suit. But he was in love for the first time in his life. He was not going to let his head over-rule his heart, when he wanted Pip with all his being as he had never wanted a woman before. He would call on her at Lady Shaw's later today and tell her that he intended to spend the rest of his life with her if she would have him.

He got up and headed for the door that led to the adjoining chamber where Harry slept. He was grinning in anticipation of seeing Harry's electrified stupor when he announced that he was going to propose to Phillipa.

He opened the door to discover his friend packing a valise which sat open on top of his unmade bed.

Devon leaned against the door frame and watched Harry while he crammed some rolled-up stockings into a corner of his traveling case.

"You have decided to go home, then," he said, for he knew Harry had wanted to return to Brookfield.

"Yes, I miss Claudia more than I thought possible. I hope to convince Mrs. Emerson to let us marry before the end of the month. Now that Petersford has made his declaration and Phillipa has accepted him, my worries on that score are over."

Devon came erect and his jaw dropped. "Miss Westhaven is marrying Francis? You're sure?"

"Yes, that is what she told me," Harry said and gazed around the room for any forgotten items. Seeing none, he secured the leather straps on his valise. He rubbed his neck and looked at Devon. "I can see that you are astounded. I, too, would have thought that Francis was quite above Pip's touch, being a marquess. And she doesn't have much of a dowry, you know. But he is plump in the pocket and doesn't need the blunt. He made it clear that he did not want some milk and water miss, which worked to Pip's advantage." His handsome lips formed into a wry grin. "I wonder if Francis knows how stubborn she can be when she has her mind set on getting her own way."

The slit of Devon's lips was a poor excuse for an answering smile, but he couldn't do better, for he felt as if someone had rammed a fist into his midsection. He schooled his features to reveal none of his inner turmoil, and the two friends took leave of one another without further mention of Phillipa.

Back in his bedchamber, Devon sank into the chair he had abandoned earlier with such elevated spirits. His inclination to berate Phillipa, who had allowed him to kiss her while she was promised to another man, was transitory. He was the expert in seduction, not her. He had lured her to the secluded lair and deliberately baited her. The transgression was his alone, not hers. Blaming Phillipa would be a rum sort of thing to do.

He would leave London for Fairlea at once, for he could not bear to see Phillipa and Petersford together and be reminded of how close he had come to making an utter fool of himself by proposing to a betrothed woman. He got up to go to the bellrope beside the fireplace to ring for his valet. But, at that moment, he was forced to respond to a knock on the bedroom door. He opened it to Ransome who stood in the hall, looking uncharacteristically nervous.

"I was about to summon you," Devon said, too absorbed in his own concerns to notice his valet's tense expression. He stood aside to let Mr. Ransome enter the room. "I leave for Fairlea within the hour, and I want you to pack for me."

Ransome did not meet the viscount's eyes, but fixed his own somewhere in the vicinity of his employer's forehead.

"My lord, I beg your pardon, but I have come to give you notice. Lord Mears was in need of a valet and offered me the position."

Devon found Ransome's decampment of small import, considering that his world had come crashing down a few minutes ago. On an ordinary day, he might have been incensed at Lord Mears's audacity in sneaking behind his back to hire away his valet, but not today.

Mr. Ransome stepped to a tall cupboard to remove the viscount's clothes, but Devon stopped him.

"Leave that," he said. "You need not come to Fairlea, Mr. Ransome. I shall give you a half-month's severance pay, for you have been an excellent servant. Go below and send James Newell up to do my packing. I am taking him to the country in your stead."

Ten

Sitting before her vanity mirror in her Brookfield bedroom, Phillipa was placing her new straw bonnet onto her brown curls. She said to Dora, who was making the bed, "Has Lord Darrington arrived from Fairlea yet?" as if it were the most unimportant question in the world.

Holding a goosedown pillow pressed firmly to her small chest, the maid replied, "No, Miss Pip, but the room where His Lordship is to change into his groomsman's clothes for Mr. Harry's wedding is ready for him."

Phillipa turned from the mirror, satisfied that the purple ribbons had been tied into a perfect bow beneath her chin. She stood up and shook out the skirts of her silk dress.

Dora paused before replacing the pillow on the bed, cocked her dark head to the side, and silently admired the lavender dress with violets embroidered at the neckline and the hem. Even after a fortnight, Dora was still unaccustomed to the sartorial splendor of the London clothes Miss Pip wore and the riot of brown curls which had transformed her everyday looks into something very special.

"You are as pretty as a bride yourself, Miss Pip," Dora murmured as she resumed her daily chore.

"Thank you, Dora," Phillipa said, amused by the wonder in the longtime servant's voice. "I had better hurry; Basil is waiting below to drive me to Mrs. Emerson's."

Phillipa was in charge of preparations for the wedding breakfast. There were some last-minute instructions she must give to the kitchen staff before driving to the village church, where Harry and Claudia were to be married this morning. But her thoughts were filled with Devon Roarke as she picked up her reticule and started toward the door.

She had experienced some very low days directly after the duchess's ball. It was customary for a gentleman to make a courtesy call on a lady after a dance, particularly if he had stood up with her or showed her some marked attention. Instead of the romantic reunion of which she had dreamed, she had suffered a hurtful snub when Devon had not been among the visitors to Lady Shaw's drawing room. In spite of her dented pride, she made excuses for him, certain he would call the next day.

"Your gloves," Dora reminded Phillipa, who turned back to retrieve them from the dresser top with an impatient gesture directed at her own forgetfulness.

She pulled on the white gloves decorated at the cuff with sprigged violets, thinking of how hopeful she had been. But Devon had never come. She had gone through periods of humiliation, self-pity, and anger. He had characterized their tryst as "not unfavorable or appalling, but quite promising." Not a roaring endorsement, but it seemed to have been sufficiently rosy to warrant his further attentions. Yet he must have had second thoughts, and found her conduct unseemly at best and wanton at worst. After all, in a male's view, in Devon's view, it was a decent female's duty to protect her reputation by roundly refusing a male's improper overtures. In his eyes, a real lady would have resisted temptation, not flung herself into his arms.

Phillipa had learned, firsthand, the bitter lesson that breach of propriety was a man's prerogative, but not a woman's. She had no desire to open herself up to Devon's cold shoulder, which would hurt. Neither was she certain that she could control her uncertain temper if he said something untoward to her.

Phillipa retraced her path to the door. She had decided days ago that even if it was cowardly, it would also be safer, all around, if she stayed out of the viscount's way today.

Phillipa sat in a pew beside Sir Nigel during the wedding ceremony in the village church. Harry, Claudia, and the blond bridesmaid who attended Phillipa's soon-to-be sister-in-law proved to be a mere blur. The vicar's words remained mostly unattended.

Phillipa feasted on Devon's handsome profile and recalled clearly the moments in the duchess's garden when love and desire had intertwined so perfectly for her. Her traitorous heart was making her light-headed. Lord help her. She still loved him. Had she no pride? If he moved his head in her direction and beckoned, she would run up to the altar and dive into his arms.

Phillipa became indebted to Sir Nigel for banishing the silly thought from her head when he nudged her with his elbow as a reminder to rise for the recessional.

Pulling herself together, she removed her gaze very

deliberately from the viscount and directed her smile more appropriately at the bride and groom.

No one questioned Phillipa's dedication when she remained in the kitchen during the wedding breakfast to ensure that the function ran smoothly. Hidden among the pots and pans, she later gazed through the scullery window when everyone crowded around the carriage which would take Claudia and Harry on their wedding trip. When the bride and groom had gone, she watched the guests climb into their own vehicles and begin to drive off.

Phillipa calculated that the coachyard would be empty in about a half an hour, and she could emerge safely from her culinary sanctuary and not run into the viscount.

But, alas, it was not to be. She turned from the window and faced Sir Nigel, who bustled through the kitchen door and said to her, "Pip, I am riding to Brookfield with Lord Krendal," naming Claudia's uncle, who had come from London for his niece's wedding. "His Lordship is a passionate horticulturist and is interested in seeing my gardens. I will leave Basil and our carriage at your disposal. Oh yes, Lord Darrington is waiting outside for you to give him a lift back to the house. I knew you wouldn't mind taking him up with you." Before she could say a word, her father was gone.

Phillipa's stomach was tied in knots when she walked toward where Devon waited for her beside the Westhaven coach. She worked to hold her head high and maintain her outward composure and suppress the unwanted sparks of love radiating through her.

Hat in hand, Devon bowed, civilly. "Miss Westhaven," he said in a matter-of-fact tone.

"Lord Darrington," she replied and inclined her head

politely, her pulse beating uncomfortably fast. He handed her up into the carriage and directed Basil to drive on.

His first words to Phillipa as the coach rolled down the country road were mere commonplaces of polite propriety about the wedding. She responded in kind and for a time they conversed like courteous strangers before he turned and stared full at her.

Initially, after losing Phillipa, Devon had tried to shut her out of his mind and forget what might have been. But, in truth, he found that even when you don't wish for love, once it happens, you are stuck with it. He had learned that it was impossible to turn off one's heart.

This morning, he found himself searching with his eyes for her at the wedding breakfast, but had been foiled by only fleeting glimpses. Now he took his fill like a thirsty man who had reached an oasis. Her face had become very dear to him. He had never tired of looking at her picture, but it was nothing like seeing the flesh and blood woman again.

Seizing on the warmth Phillipa was sure she saw in Devon's blue eyes, she took a chance and raised their meaningless discourse to what was really on her mind.

"Harry mentioned that Miss Kiernon is engaged to marry Lord Mears. I thought that you and she . . ." The words dangled uncertainly, her courage faltering slightly.

To her surprise, Devon chuckled.

"Marilee did a darned sight better than a mere viscount. Mears commands a dukedom, you know." He did not feel obligated to mention the brotherly heart-to-heart talk he had had with the little beauty which had pointed her in Lord Mears's direction.

Emboldened by her interest in his marital prospects,

Devon asked the one question to which *he* badly wanted an answer.

"Harry said you were becoming betrothed to Marilee's cousin Francis. Is the happy announcement still pending?"

She shook her head. "I will not bore you with chapter and verse, but, although I almost talked myself into accepting Lord Petersford's proposal, for he is a fine gentleman, I thought better of it."

Devon's heart lightened as he began to size up the situation. The wall that had kept him from courting Phillipa appeared to be coming down. She was not in love with Francis Kiernon, but that did not necessarily mean that she loved him. He would not rush into another rash decision where she was concerned, for he was in no shape to go through a second rejection.

"Harry must have been disappointed when you turned down a marquess," he said with a small laugh.

Phillipa gave him a cunning smirk. "Oh yes. He was blue-deviled until he learned that I had decided to accept Lady Shaw's offer to live with her. I won't be intruding on Harry and his bride by remaining here at Brookfield. My aunt is alone often in London with Lord Shaw in the diplomatic corps, and desires me to provide her company."

The coach came to a stop. Devon alighted and handed Phillipa down.

Inside the house he said, "Excuse me, ma'am, but I must change into my traveling clothes," and made for the stairs.

"You won't leave without saying good-bye?" Phillipa called after him when he was halfway to the second floor.

He turned. "Of course not," he said. He took the

remaining steps two at time and was soon from her sight.

When Phillipa heard footsteps coming down the hall, she turned in the direction of the servant's wing to see who was approaching.

"James," she hailed the young valet as he came forward and stood beside her with a wide smile on his ingenuous face.

Phillipa spun him around, admired the tailoring of his fine black coat, and made much of his new status.

"My, how you have come up in the world. Imagine! James Newell—the personal valet of a lord."

"Stop, Miss Pip, or you will give me airs," James implored, a little embarrassed. "Did I hear His Lordship's voice just now?"

"Yes, he has gone to ready himself for the trip back to Fairlea."

"I had best go up," James said. He put one black shoe onto the bottom rung of the stairs, but paused in his ascent and turned to Phillipa. "Something has baffled me ever since I went into service for the viscount, Miss Pip."

"What is that?"

"Do you and His Lordship have an understanding?"

"An understanding? Good gracious, James, what makes you ask such a question?"

"Lord Darrington keeps a picture he drew of you in a frame on his bedside table. The rendering of your face is the first thing His Lordship sees when he awakens in the morning and the last thing on which he gazes before he extinguishes his candle for the night."

Overcome with a paralysis of disbelief, Phillipa stared openmouthed at James.

"Have I put my foot wrong mentioning Lord Darrington's admiration for you?"

Phillipa broke off her stupefied stare. "No, James. I am glad to know it. Go on up to His Lordship."

Overwhelming relief swept through Phillipa. Devon loved her. She began to pace back and forth in front of the staircase. Something had gone wrong that caused him to think that she did not care for him. What it was, she did not know. When he came down, should she confess to him that she loved him now that she knew he was like-minded? Society dictated that a gentleman should be the first to declare his feelings. Dare she go against convention and make the first move? Dare she not?

Phillipa was carrying on a running conversation with herself when the subject of her polemics appeared at the top of the staircase and started down. She knew she must do something. She might have been less frantic had she known that the viscount hoarded an advantage over her.

Devon was armed with Newell's confession that he, James, had revealed to Miss Pip that His Lordship kept her picture on his bedside table. How Phillipa used the knowledge, Devon thought, would determine their future. It was in her hands. If she did not love him, she would be embarrassed and say nothing. But if Pip loved him . . . the sentence remained unfinished.

He heard her say, "I must speak with you, Devon." His spirits soared, for she apparently cared, or she would not have used his given name. But he had no intention of jumping the gun. He followed Phillipa to a small visitors' anteroom off the vestibule and closed the door to ensure their privacy.

He pulled out a chair from the wall, and Phillipa slid

down onto it. Devon lowered himself into a second chair, which he positioned facing her with his knees nearly touching hers.

Evading his gaze, Phillipa stared at the crimson rug beneath their feet. "I don't know how to begin," she said.

"Why not with the truth?"

She lifted her head and looked straight at him. "James said you keep a picture of me on your bedside table."

"What have you concluded from that, my dear?"

"I can't imagine what it means," she said softly, but her quibbling lacked conviction.

Devon brought her hand to his cheek and held it there. "Come, Pip, let us have no more roundaboutation. Enlighten me."

"It seems that you love me as much as I love you. But what happened, Devon? I waited for days after the duchess's ball for you to come to me, before I gave up all hope when I learned that you had left London."

He sighed deeply. "I went to Harry to declare my intentions to make you my wife, but before I could say anything, he informed me that you were betrothed to Petersford. I can tell you, Pip, hearing that was like a dash of cold water. There was no way that I could trespass on another man's preserve."

Phillipa groaned. "It seems life can be altered by one twinkling of foolishness. In a weak moment, I said to Harry that I would accept Francis's offer. That was before you kissed me and I knew I loved you," she said. "When the marquess came back to Town from his estate, I told him that we could not make a match."

For a time they looked at each other until Phillipa broke the short silence. "It will be all right now, won't it, Devon?"

His expression was pensive. "I suppose you wouldn't consider tossing Mary Wollstonecraft's tome into the fire some cold night."

"Burn a book?" She looked startled.

Devon leaned over and kissed her lightly. "I was joking, sweetheart." He sighed again. "I love you, Pip, and I want to marry you. But are you certain that is what *you* want? I am not a man who would tolerate petticoat rule or suffer a wife who would constantly fly in the face of my wishes. I wouldn't want us forever clashing."

"Nor would I be content with a spineless man who would allow himself to be dominated by me, my lord. Although I cannot promise to be a meek mate, I will not seek to rule you."

"You are sure that you want to marry me?"

"Very sure. Mary Wollstonecraft had some interesting ideas, but contrary to what you may think, her book is not my bible. You and I together will create our own blueprint for a happy marriage which will suit both of us."

His answering smile was agreeable. "I, too, may have misled you, you know. I am not a great fan of infidelity and would never insult you by taking a mistress. You, sweetheart, shall always be my one and only love."

Phillipa looked at him adoringly. "Devon Roarke, you are the most wonderful man in the world."

His grin became waggish. "And you, my darling, are a very discerning woman. But enough of this unbosoming. Let us seek out Sir Nigel and make our engagement official and set a wedding date. June, in the chapel in the rose garden, wasn't it to be?"

"You remembered!" Ridiculously happy, Phillipa pitched forward into his arms and kissed him soundly.

Epilogue

The wedding during the second week in June was as picture perfect as any romantic could wish. The sun shone warm and bright in the rose garden outside Brookfield chapel, which was decorated within with porcelain bowls of pink and white roses set in deep recesses about the church. The aisle of the sanctuary was strewn with rose petals in romantic profusion.

Phillipa wore a silk dress of the palest pink and a crown of pink and white roses on her dark curls. Devon was smartly dressed in black breeches and a white linen coat with a pink rosebud in the top buttonhole. Claudia and Harry attended the happy couple. The small church was packed to overflowing with guests.

During the exchange of vows, Lady Shaw sobbed happily into her Chantilly lace handkerchief. Sir Nigel brushed a sentimental tear from his round cheek. And Lord Charing looked on, pleased with his only son's choice of a bride. Sitting in a back pew was James Newell. He appeared decidedly smug when the vicar pronounced Miss Pip and the viscount, man and wife, for he was very sure that were it not for his clever interference this wedding would never have taken place.

THE JUNE BRIDE CONSPIRACY

Regina Scott

Although no records have been found of a "Secret Service" during the Regency, that period seems to demand the kind of charming spy immortalized by Ian Fleming's James Bond. Enter Harold Petersborough, Marquis of Hastings, and his cadre of peers. Though his office is my own invention, I feel he and his men are true to the excitement and elegance that was the Regency. To them and the men like them I dedicate this book.

Books by Regina Scott

The Unflappable Miss Fairchild

The Twelve Days of Christmas

"Sweeter Than Candy" in A Match for Mother

The Bluestocking on His Knee

Catch of the Season

"A Place by the Fire" in Mistletoe Kittens

A Dangerous Dalliance

The Marquis's Kiss

Coming in July 2001

The Incomparable Miss Compton

One

Lady Abigail Lindby took one look at the selection of roses in the florist's shop on New Bond Street and burst into tears for the third time that morning.

Joanna Lindby smiled indulgently, tucking a stray black hair back under her fashionable chip bonnet before reaching out to give her mother's plump hands a squeeze.

"I'm to be married," she explained to the deferent and dismayed florist, "in June."

The florist, a tall man as thin and pale as the calla lilies in his shop window, obviously understood. "Many happy returns, my lady," he warbled. "And may I say that roses are an excellent choice."

"No, no," Lady Lindby fussed, sniffing back her tears and shaking her head so vigorously that she set the ostrich plumes on her broad-brimmed bonnet to quivering. "Roses are so ordinary. Mrs. Winterhouse had them for her daughter Belinda and the two of them never slept together."

The florist blinked in obvious confusion.

"What she means," Joanna put in quickly from long practice, "is that unless one puts as much planning into a wedding as a marriage, the husband and wife may not be as congenial toward each other as they ought."

Now her mother blinked. "Isn't that what I said? There is no need to belabor the issue, dear. Now, as I was saying, something more exotic. What do you think of India, young man?"

Joanna's smile deepened. Her mother was notorious among the *ton* for her unique brand of conversation. Her round face and equally round frame, along with small, wide-set eyes and a rosebud mouth, combined to make people think she was dim. In reality, Lady Lindby was quite intelligent. She simply couldn't stop the rapid flight of her thoughts long enough to put together coherent conversations. After years of practice, Joanna found it easy to guess what was on her mother's mind. Now she managed to order several simple arrangements for the wedding breakfast from the befuddled florist and extract her mother from the shop without further ado.

As they rejoined their already laden liveried footman and continued their walk up New Bond Street, they had to stop every few moments to accept additional congratulations from various acquaintances. The weather was chill for early May. Joanna hugged her blue satin pelisse to her and wished she'd thought to wear a shawl over the top as her mother had done with her own serpentine satin pelisse. Yet as she was forced to smile and offer her thanks for each fervent wish for her happiness, she began to wonder whether it was the weather or her situation she found uncomfortable.

Surely this uneasiness she felt was only the prewedding jitters of any bride. She nodded at Lady Wentworth's advice on household management and promised Genevieve Munroe that she would be one of the bridesmaids. Her mother managed to call everyone by their correct names and remembered to thank them for their kind thoughts. It should all have been very endearing but by the time they reached the dressmaker's several shops down, Joanna could feel her smile becoming strained.

"And how might we serve madam today?" the heavy-set dressmaker sang out, rushing forward in a cloud of lilac perfume.

"Yellow," Lady Lindby pronounced. "Though not a bright shade. I would not want Joanna to blind the fellow before she got him home."

"That is to say," Joanna supplied hurriedly as the dressmaker frowned in confusion, "my mother would like a gown in an understated tone. I am to be married, in June."

Of course, more congratulations followed; however, Joanna was glad when the woman led her to a velvet upholstered seat before a mirrored dressing table.

"Cream is all the rage," the dressmaker confided, removing Joanna's bonnet, "but with your coloring, I'd try for something more dramatic."

She draped a swatch of silver white satin over the shoulders of Joanna's pelisse. The color enhanced her pale skin and brought out the shine in her thick black hair. Above the swatch, her dark eyes glowed warmly.

"I have just the lace for it," the dressmaker continued. "In the finest Brussels rose pattern with silver embroidery. It will match that lovely diamond ring of yours. You'll be more regal than a queen. He won't be able to take his eyes off you."

As her mother stepped forward to discuss design and fittings, Joanna glanced down at the heavy diamond engagement ring, twisting it about her finger. She had been so happy when Allister had slipped it on her hand. Yet somehow in the days that had followed, clouds had crossed the sunshine of her delight. She was now certain that the design of her wedding dress would make little difference. Allister found it all too easy to take his eyes off her. She was afraid the wedding would not change that.

Walking back to their carriage with her mother, she scolded herself for her lack of confidence. She should be thankful. No one had ever expected her to make such a brilliant match. Oh, she had had suitors. Her dark coloring and elegant figure had guaranteed that she would be sought out. But that same composure, coupled with a shy nature, had deterred close connections. Her widowed mother had begged her to try harder, but she couldn't seem to do so. Consequently, she had earned the reputation of being cold.

Yet she knew nothing could be further from the truth. A passionate heart beat in her breast. She had simply waited for the right man with whom to share it.

Enter Allister Fenwick, Baron Trevithan. One could not ask for a more likely hero. His hair was as dark and thick as hers, and wavier, swept back from a square-jawed face. His deep-set eyes were chips of sapphire that warmed with his mood. His figure was trim; he prowled with the grace of an African predator. To top it all off, he was something of a mystery, having been on assignment to the War Office since graduating from Oxford ten years ago. That this dark and dangerous lord should show interest in her was beyond anything she could have imagined. Yet the first time she had danced with him, she'd known he could unlock the door of her heart; after a month of courting she had been willing to hand him the key. The day he had proposed had been the happiest day of her life.

Except . . .

He had yet to introduce her to any of his friends.

While it seemed many people knew *of* him, few *knew* him. She could not help but wonder whether there was something amiss that so perfect a specimen of manhood would have so few intimates.

Except . . .

She could not seem to keep his interest when discussing wedding plans. A certain reticence on the part of the groom was to be expected; in her experience, gentlemen seldom cared about the details of decoration and deportment the way a lady did. But she couldn't help noticing that there were moments when she was talking to him about more serious subjects and his eyes would dim. If she questioned him he could answer readily enough, but she had the impression that his thoughts were elsewhere.

Except . . .

He hadn't told her he loved her. She'd been so brazen as to ask him outright once, but his smile and wink in response had only been momentarily satisfying. Oh, it wasn't that he was indifferent. He demonstrated a kind consideration whenever they were together. And certainly she had no complaint for his romantic abilities. He sent her flowers, he took her for long walks and held her hand, he waltzed with her more often than was strictly proper, and he stole kisses at flatteringly frequent intervals. In fact, the touch of his lips to hers raised a tempest inside her that usually resulted in a swollen mouth, tousled hair, and a satisfied smile on His Lordship's handsome face. But not once had he seemed so affected.

As they alighted from the carriage and climbed the stairs to the cheery red door of their small stone town house off Grosvenor Square, Joanna sighed. Perhaps she had no confidence in his devotion because they had only known each other a short time. He had only courted her for three months before proposing, after all. Three months was a very short time to feel comfortable with a situation. She'd lived in the trim three-story town house since her father had died eight years ago and it still felt stiff and cold to her, for all that her mother had decorated it in shades of yellow and bought many fine paintings and porcelains to enhance it. If she took so long to welcome change, she could not expect Allister to change his bachelor ways so quickly. She had to remember that he *had* proposed—that was the important thing. While he might not love her as deeply as she loved him, they had time. She had every confidence that she would make him a good wife. Perhaps, with time and proximity, he would lose his heart more fully.

"So much to do," her mother lamented as they entered the marble-tiled foyer. "We've only gotten out the first batch of invitations. The family is already sending presents. My friends are clambering to know if they may throw parties for you. This wedding will be the death of me as long as I live."

"I promise I'll be right there to help, Mother," Joanna assured her. Pausing by the half-moon hall table, she thumbed through the stack of cards and invitations that had arrived in their absence. One cream-colored note stood out from the others on the brass tray. It was addressed to her mother, and the sealing wax bore no signet.

"What could this be?" she asked her mother.

Lady Lindby handed her reticule and spencer to the waiting elderly butler and crossed to her daughter's side. Raising an eyebrow, she took the note and opened it. As her button brown eyes moved down the page, all color drained from her face. Joanna watched in alarm as her mother collapsed into the Hepplewhite chair beside the table.

"Mother!" she cried, kneeling in front of her. "Ames, get the smelling salts from my mother's dressing table."

As the butler hurried away, her mother moaned. "Oh, my poor heart." She stared off into the distance. Tears sparkled again, but Joanna knew they could not be from joy. Her mother focused on her with difficulty. "Oh, my poor Joanna!"

"Mother, what is it?" she begged, taking the nearest hand in her own. The short fingers were cold in her grip.

Her mother held out the note with her other hand. "I'm so sorry, dearest."

"Allister?" Joanna gasped in realization. "Has something happened to Allister?" She snatched the letter from her mother's trembling fingers, rising to scan it.

"Lady Lindby," it read in a firm masculine hand, *"it is with great distress and after many hours of consideration that I must rescind my offer for your daughter. I find I am simply not ready to embark on the sea of matrimony. I wish you luck in the future."* It was signed merely "Trevithan."

Joanna felt cold to the center of her being. How could he? Had she been so uninteresting that she could be summarily dismissed? How could he end their engagement with this disgustingly inadequate note? How could he send such a message to her mother, in such a cowardly fashion? How could he offer no honorable reason, no acceptable excuse for putting them through such embarrassment, such pain? Did he think she was without sensibility, without feeling?

"Oh, my poor dear," her mother moaned, gazing up

at her with tears staining pale cheeks. "What will we do?"

"Do?" Joanna asked with a cold fury. "Do? Oh, I promise you, madam, we will do something. This is insufferable. Unthinkable." She drew herself up to her full height and glared at her mother, the gaping footman, and the butler who had just returned with the smelling salts.

"I will be married," she swore, "in June."

Two

Allister Fenwick, Baron Trevithan, generally did not have second thoughts. He had lived too long in a world of split-second decisions. One made a choice with the best information available and either reaped the rewards or paid the consequences. Now that he had chosen to leave that world behind, it only remained to be seen which result it would be this time. He had every expectation and hope that with Joanna Lindby, he had found his reward at last.

"Then you're certain I can't entice you into coming back to the Service?" Davis asked.

Allister eyed his longtime friend and partner as they sat in the sparsely furnished flat Allister had rented in London. Despite ten years of intense work, Davis Laughton still looked like a newly graduated Oxford scholar in his simple brown coat and trousers. His round boyish face, soft brown hair, and large liquid brown eyes habitually caused the enemies of the Crown to underestimate him. Behind his innocent facade lurked a keen mind and a determined spirit. No doubt those traits had been what had induced Lord Hastings to recruit him along with Allister into His Majesty's Secret Service immediately after they left college. For many years, neither had regretted it. The excitement and challenge had been more than enough to compensate for loss of family and friends.

Until recently.

"Sorry, old chap," Allister said with true regret, crossing the legs of his chamois trousers. "It's time to hang up the sword."

"If you quote me the verse about ploughshares, I shall demand brandy," Davis threatened. "In fact, I may demand a brandy anyway. Are you really intent on leaving me to go it alone?"

Allister grimaced. "They'll give you a new partner. Lord Hastings already has several candidates."

"Untried steeds," Davis complained. "And I get the dubious pleasure of breaking them in."

"We were young, once," Allister reminded him. "We turned out all right."

"Well, one of us did," Davis joked. Then his dark eyes clouded. "Seriously, Trev, I'm going to miss you. Are you sure this Lindby chit is worth it?"

"She isn't a chit," he corrected his friend. "Joanna Lindby is a diamond of the first water. She is well bred, well educated, and well respected. I am the most fortunate of men."

Davis sighed. "I was afraid of that. I had a feeling you were smitten the first time you pointed her out across the room. You had a look in your eye I'd never seen before. I envy you."

Allister felt himself squirm internally under the praise, though he was too well trained to allow it to show in his demeanor. Joanna was everything he had claimed to Davis, and more, but he was acutely aware that his feelings did not do her justice. He knew it was no fault of the lovely Joanna. Her midnight black tresses, thick and lustrous, framed an oval, high-cheekboned face. Her skin was like alabaster, her eyes dark and soulful. Her figure was willowy and elegant, with just enough curves to set a fellow dreaming of what lay beneath the fashionable silk gowns she wore. She was modest and soft-spoken, intelligent and gracious. That this virtuous paragon should agree to his proposal was the best for which he could have hoped. The first time he had danced with her he'd known she was special, and after a month of courting he was certain she'd make the perfect wife. The day she had accepted his proposal had been the happiest day of his life.

Except . . .

He wasn't sure how honest he was capable of being with her. He had spent the last ten years of his life pretending. He'd been a carter, a courtier, a coachman, and a Comte. He'd had to hide his thoughts, his opinions, his feelings. Could he now learn to share them openly as was required for a good marriage?

Except . . .

He wondered whether he could live the life other men of his class seemed to live. Could he settle down to a life with no more excitement than watching prices on the Exchange and visiting White's? Courting had held a certain charm; it was a bit like matching wits with the enemy. But once life moved to happily ever after, would he be satisfied with his lot?

Except . . .

He wondered what kind of husband he'd make. He had never had a proper relationship with a woman. Any other lady had been wooed either in the service of his country or to forget it. Both types had seemed rather pleased with his abilities; certainly he had never had any complaints. And by the way Joanna kissed him, full of innocent fire, there would be no passion lacking from her side. Still, she was a proper young lady and what he felt for her was far superior to anything he had felt before. He just wasn't certain what he felt was love.

"Is it Daremier?" Davis asked quietly.

Allister started. "The Skull? Certainly not. Why would you ask?"

"Silly question," Davis quipped. "Why would I ask about an arch French spy who's been a thorn in your side for years? I'm certain I'm the only one who has noticed your retirement from the Service coincides with him besting you. Shall I warm the fire for you? Would you like the covers turned back for your afternoon nap?"

"The sarcasm is unamusing," Allister informed him. "Need I remind you that I can still beat you with either sword or pistol?"

Davis's eyes lighted, and he leaned forward eagerly. "No reminder necessary. You are the best. And you could prove that if you'd only come back to the Service."

Allister shook his head but before he could refuse again, the temporary man-of-all-work he had hired gave a cough in the doorway. A tall man with a long face, he had struck Allister as the type who would do his work and ask no questions.

"Yes, Patterson?" he asked.

"There's a lady to see you, sir," he intoned, keeping his eyes humbly downcast. Only the severe set to his wide mouth told of his disapproval at this state of affairs.

Davis hopped to his feet. "You old fraud, you! And I was worried you'd collapsed into propriety. Who is she, old chap? And does she have a friend?"

"I haven't had a woman since I started courting

Joanna," Allister told him icily. He returned his gaze to his servant. "Does this lady have a name, Patterson?"

"A Miss Joanna Lindby," the man replied with no more enthusiasm.

Allister leapt to his feet, pulse roaring in his ears. "Joanna? Something must be wrong."

Davis stepped to his side and put a hand on his arm to keep him from running from the room. "Easy, lad. She probably just wants to confirm the flowers for the wedding or some such frippery. Tell the lady to come in, my man."

Allister managed a shaky laugh as Patterson hurried from the room. Why had he reacted that way? He'd been cooler two years ago when Lord Hastings had informed him that Davis had been shot. Besides, his friend was no doubt right. If something had happened to Joanna, it would have been her mother who would have contacted him, and probably by note. The fact that Joanna felt comfortable enough to approach him in residence should reassure him that they were becoming closer.

One look at her face had the opposite effect. She was flushed, her jaw set, and her eyes sparked fire.

He met her just inside the door. "Joanna, what is it?"

She raised a haughty eyebrow. "Didn't you expect me to ask for an explanation?" she demanded. "Do you think so little of me?"

"What are you talking about?" He frowned. "An explanation for what?"

"Perhaps I should go," Davis muttered, picking up his top hat from the side table between the two chairs.

"Forgive my manners," Allister apologized to them both. "Miss Joanna Lindby, may I present my friend, Mr. Davis Laughton."

Davis bowed. "Your servant, madam."

Joanna glared at him, offering no more than a nod. "Good day, sir."

His friend swallowed. "Yes, well, as I said. I should go."

"Don't leave on my account," she clipped out. "This should only take a moment." She faced Allister again, and he could only marvel at the fire in her. He had thought her passionate, but had never suspected she could be so intense. He was not a little surprised to find it intrigued him.

"I only want to know why," she said to him. "Why did you choose to break off our engagement?"

Allister stared at her. "Break off our engagement? What would make you think I'd do a thing like that?"

"Oh, I don't know," she sneered. "Perhaps because of this?" She flung a note at him, and he caught it against the chest of his white lawn shirt. Instinct told him not to take his eyes off her, but he had to know what had so incensed her. He scanned the contents of the note and felt his blood run cold.

"What is it?" Davis asked at his elbow.

"Here," Allister said, thrusting it at him. "Read it." As Davis glanced at the paper, Allister returned his gaze to his intended. "Joanna, I assure you, I didn't send that note. I want nothing more than to be your husband."

Her eyes probed his as if seeking the truth. He returned her gaze steadfastly. He'd made viscounts and villains believe him when needed. Surely now that he spoke the truth he would be even more convincing. Joanna held his gaze for a moment, then looked away.

"I wish I could believe that," she murmured.

Could she see inside him to his doubts of his adequacy? He had to convince them both. Allister caught her hands. "Believe it, for it is the truth," he told her fervently. "I would never hurt you like this. If we had a disagreement, I'd like to think we could discuss it. I would never simply send a note dismissing you."

Tears sprang to her eyes, and he reached up a hand to stroke them away from her soft skin. She swallowed.

"Oh, Allister, I'm so glad. When I saw that horrid note, all I could think was that you didn't care."

He felt his jaw tighten as her pain pierced his heart. "That's exactly what someone wanted you to think."

"But why?" she asked with a frown. "Who'd want to hurt us?"

Allister exchanged glances with Davis. There was a grim set to his friend's mouth that told Allister he had similar thoughts. Despite the fact that he should be worried about the matter, he felt the familiar tingle of excitement that always came with a mystery.

"I have no idea," he said to Joanna. "But I intend to find out."

Three

Joanna should have felt nothing but relief. Allister still wanted to marry her. His murmured reassurances and protective caresses as he escorted her home in her carriage should have soothed her fears. When he took her in his arms and kissed away the last of her tears, she could only melt against him in bliss.

But something was wrong. Someone was trying to pull them apart. By the way he had exchanged looks with his friend, he knew more than he wanted to tell her. She had a feeling she was about to confront his supposedly dangerous past, and she wasn't sure what to do about it.

He was diplomacy itself, coming in to placate and reassure her mother, then inviting them both to the opera the next evening to make up for their difficult afternoon. As Joanna walked him to the door, he brought her hand to his lips and pressed a fervent kiss into her palm.

"I'll let you know as soon as I hear anything," he promised.

"Can you tell me what you suspect?" she pleaded. "I can't think of anyone who would be so vindictive."

"I'm sure it's no one you know," he replied.

"But you suspect it's someone you know, don't you?"

He did not accept her challenge. "I don't want you to worry. I promise I'll get to the bottom of this. It may take me some time, so don't be concerned if you don't see me before tomorrow."

The fact that he seemed rather excited about the matter did nothing to reassure her.

She tried, however, to put the incident from her mind as she went about her wedding preparations the rest of the day. Her mother's spirits were fully restored, and she threw herself back into the work. They had a number of critical decisions to make, chief among them who would escort her down the aisle since her own father had been dead for many years. After a lengthy discussion, they decided to ask her Uncle Mervyn, who had always been close. They then spent the evening addressing invitations from the lengthy list her mother had compiled. It was when they finished with her family and friends and prepared to start Allister's list that she felt the uneasiness return.

"He still hasn't given me a list," her mother complained. "Think, dearest. He must have told you someone to invite besides his cousins in Somerset. Was he found under a cabbage leaf?"

Joanna smiled. "Most likely not. However, he told me his parents are dead. I believe he has an uncle somewhere."

"Well, I'm glad I've at least invited his cousins, the Darbys," her mother replied. "I remember him mentioning them. Was he directly related to the old earl or the new earl? Or is it the newer earl? That family changes its mind so quickly."

"I'm not certain," Joanna replied, realizing again how little she knew about her intended. "But we should add a Mr. Davis Laughton to the list. I met him today. He appears to be a particular friend of Allister's."

"Davis Laughton," her mother mused. "Where have I heard that name before?"

"Have you heard it before?" Joanna asked eagerly.

Her mother shook her head. "No, I don't believe so. Which does seem odd, for I know everyone, even if I can't remember a name at a given moment."

Joanna nodded. For all her mother's eccentricities, she was well liked among the *ton*. An interesting person was always welcome, and her mother had never lacked for acquaintances. If Davis Laughton had lived in London for any length of time, it would have been surprising that her mother had never heard of him.

"Perhaps he's up from the country," Joanna suggested.

"Yes, of course," her mother agreed. "In which case you must ask him when he's returning. What's the postage to Africa?"

"Uncle Mervyn will be back from Africa before you need to send the invitation," Joanna assured her, once again interpreting her mother's remark. She promised her mother to check into the matter of Mr. Laughton's address, although in truth she wasn't certain she'd have an opportunity to talk to Mr. Laughton again. Allister generally didn't make a party of their outings, seeming to prefer to keep her all to himself. She resolved to ask him about his friend when they went to the opera the next evening. And she would ask him about whom else to invite as well.

If Joanna had a difficult afternoon, Allister's was far worse.

"That's the lot of them, my friend," Harold Peters-borough, Marquis of Hastings, had informed him as they sat in his spacious private suite at the War Office. "Every assassin, spy, or miscreant you ever went after is either in prison or dead, except one."

"Daremier," Allister spat.

"Daremier," Lord Hastings agreed. "A slippery fellow, that one. We still haven't learned how he manages to return to England undetected. One would think that face of his would give him away."

Allister glanced down at Lord Hastings's claw-footed desk, on which lay the charcoal sketch that was all most of His Lordship's operatives had to go on. He didn't need it. He'd seen the face too often, right before losing it again. There was good reason France's top spy was called The Skull. Deep-set, nearly black eyes looked out over prominent cheekbones and a hooked nose. Coupled with a bald pate and a cruel mouth, the face was one to give nightmares. It was also one easily disguised. That was one of the reasons Daremier was difficult to catch. The other was that he was cunningly ruthless. Nothing and no one stood in the way of his target. If The Skull had sent the note, Joanna was in danger.

"Do you think he'll hurt her?" Allister asked with a mouth gone suddenly dry.

"Your bride-to-be?" Hastings returned, stroking his walrus mustache. "Doubtful. He generally hasn't gone for revenge. The dastard's too busy with his next operation."

Allister glanced at his former supervisor. Hastings had been a senior agent at the time he had recruited Allister and Davis ten years ago. The offer had been made in this very office, as Allister stood on the same thick blue carpet, gazing across the heavy desk at the man behind it. Hastings had been trim and wiry then, an intense light burning behind his deep-set brown eyes. Now his thick, short-cropped hair was a solid iron gray, as was his mustache. Lines etched his eyes and mobile mouth. The only thing that hadn't changed was his energy. Hastings was efficient to a fault. Allister had never before had cause to question him. He felt a little guilty doing so now, but he had to know the worst of it.

"Do we know where Daremier is?" he pressed, unwilling to accept an easy solution to the problem of the note. He'd followed The Skull too long; there were too many grudges, on both sides. "Has he been sighted in England?"

"Not recently," Hastings confirmed. "But that means nothing. We seldom know where the fellow is going to strike until he's gone and struck."

Allister's eyes narrowed. "True. So, instead of trying to find him, why don't we get him to come to us?"

"A trap?" Hastings shrugged in his well-fitted navy coat. "We've tried before. He wasn't interested in those counterfeit battle plans we hid so well. Lady de Renard wouldn't let us use the Sebastien diamonds."

"Ah," Allister said, "but we have something he wants far more than Wellington's battle plans or the biggest diamonds in France."

Hastings frowned. "What?"

Allister smiled tightly. "Me."

Hastings's frown deepened, and he eyed Allister thoughtfully. "You love her that much, do you?"

Allister paused. Only that day he had been thinking his love was not deep enough for a true marriage. Even now, he could not deny that his reasons for wanting to catch the French spy had just as much to do with their long history as his devotion to Joanna.

Hastings obviously took his silence for agreement. "He won't spare you if you go in unarmed," he warned. "We may catch him, but we'd certainly lose you. I can't take that chance with your life. Let's give the lads a few more days. We don't even know he's in England."

"Someone sent that note," Allister reminded him. "And I won't rest until he's uncovered and stopped."

He was soon to know the truth of that statement. He had always been a light sleeper, a fact that had saved his life more than once. Yet, despite his sometimes dangerous circumstances, he had never had nightmares. Dreams, certainly, but nothing that made him wake up at all concerned. It was as if his mind knew, even asleep, that he had done the best he could.

That night was horrifying. In dream after dream he tried for something he could not attain. Once it was Davis, who had fallen out of the smuggler's boat they used to cross to France. He watched, helpless, as his friend was swept away by an angry sea. Another time it was his father and mother, who had died of the influenza when he was in college. In the dream, they stood behind bars and pleaded with him to release them. But the worst dream involved Joanna. In it, he saw The Skull holding her at knifepoint and laughing as he plunged the dagger into her heart. The accusation in her eyes haunted him even after he jerked awake, crying her name.

He barreled into the War Office the next day, ready to battle anyone who disagreed with his ideas about capturing The Skull. He was disappointed to find that Lord Hastings was out, and Davis was nowhere to be found.

Frustrated, he pored over the reports of the last few encounters with The Skull, groaning aloud when he saw how easily the fellow evaded them. Why had he thought he could simply retire from all this? Even if he could have quelled the pounding of his pulse, he could not deny that Daremier had to be stopped.

If no one else would do it, it was up to him.

Four

As it turned out, Joanna didn't have to worry about
whether she would see Davis Laughton again. Ames announced him that afternoon as she and her mother were
working on her trousseau in their sitting room. Her
mother hastily bundled up the frilly lace underthings
they had been stitching and hurried them from the sunny
little room. That left Joanna with a few minutes alone
with the man.

He bowed over her hand and seated himself on the
edge of a nearby Chippendale, brown-coated elbows
tight against the curving arms of the polished chair. She
had not done more than glance at him when they had
met in Allister's flat. Now she considered him more
carefully from her place on the primrose-patterned sofa,
noting the youthful face and wiry body. He would be
easy to take for a scholar, or a young solicitor. But
beneath the boyish exterior, she felt a confidence and
tension that bespoke an older, more experienced man.

"Is everything all right with Allister?" she couldn't
help asking when he did no more than exchange pleasantries.

"Yes, he's fine," he assured her. "He asked me to
stop by and check on you. I take it everything is fine
here as well?"

So, that was his agenda. Allister was trying to determine whether she'd had any more contact with their mysterious note writer. "I have nothing to report," she told him, smoothing down the skirts of her greensprigged muslin gown.

He blinked as if surprised by her choice of words, then offered her a polite smile. "Lord Trevithan also wanted you to know that he may have to postpone your outing this evening."

Disappointment shot through her, at both the situation and Allister. "I thought we had agreed that he would bring me bad news himself."

He returned her gaze without squirming. "I did not say the event was canceled, only potentially postponed. I'm sure he didn't see that as such terrible news."

No, she thought, *he probably didn't. That is entirely the problem.* "Forgive my disappointment, Mr. Laughton," she said aloud. "It is always sad to hear I shall be deprived of my betrothed's company. Thank you for troubling yourself to deliver the message. As you are obviously a particular friend of Allister's, I'm sure he would want me to invite you to the wedding. Where shall I have my mother address the invitation?"

His smile was pleasant, but it did not reach his eyes. "Don't trouble yourself. Just give the invitation to Lord Trevithan and I'm sure he'll see that I receive it."

A singular request, but she supposed it was reasonable, particularly if he were staying in a hotel with unreliable post service. "I'll do that then," she replied. "How is Allister today? I trust his search goes well?"

"Search, madam?" he asked innocently.

"For the writer of that note," she explained, then she frowned. "That is what keeps Allister from my side, is it not?"

He pursed his lips, eyeing her. "May I speak frankly, Miss Lindby?"

"I wish someone would!" Joanna told him.

"Very well." He inched forward in the chair and locked gazes with her. Joanna felt herself lean forward as well.

"I'm sure Lord Trevithan has told you that he works for the War Office. I work there as well. It can be a dangerous job, Miss Lindby, to us personally and, sadly, often to those we love. Lord Trevithan has made a number of enemies over the years. It is not surprising that one of them seeks to ruin his chance at happiness."

Joanna swallowed. "Goodness! Is this person dangerous? Homicidal?"

He rose, and she rose with him. "One would certainly hope not. However, it is possible. Lord Trevithan will no doubt do everything in his power to protect you, but there is always the slightest of chances that he will fail. I thought you should be warned."

"Yes, yes, of course," Joanna mumbled, mind churning. Dark and dangerous was one thing. Deadly was quite another. What had her impetuous heart gotten her into? Was she in danger? Was her mother in danger? Would Allister be harmed trying to protect them?

Her thoughts must have been written on her face, for Davis took a step closer, dark eyes glittering.

"Under the circumstances, Miss Lindby," he said, "I think Lord Trevithan would understand if you wanted to call off the wedding."

Call off the wedding?

She stared at him. Perhaps some would have said that was the wisest course. She did not consider herself a particularly brave person. Surely if she called off the wedding she would be safe. She would not be a target if she were not connected with Allister. And she would not have to worry about whether she could keep his attention throughout their marriage. But to call off the wedding when even a homicidal madman saw that Allister cared for her enough to be concerned? To forgo the excitement of his kiss, the joy of his presence in her life? She shook her head.

"No, Mr. Laughton," she replied firmly. "I will not call off the wedding. I will be married, in June."

Allister was almost afraid to see Joanna that night, yet he longed to hold her in his arms and prove to himself that she was all right. After changing into his evening black and taking a quick dinner, he walked the short distance to Mayfair to meet her and her mother.

As bright as a bluebird in her sapphire silk evening gown, Lady Lindby fluttered in to join him in the sitting room after the butler had admitted him.

"Oh, Lord Trevithan," she panted. "I'm so sorry to have to tell you this."

Allister was on his feet instantly, heart hammering. "What? Is it Joanna? What's happened?"

She stopped abruptly, blinking. "Why, nothing. I merely wished to apologize that she isn't ready. She seemed to be under the impression that you weren't coming."

"Was there another note?" he asked tightly.

"No, no," she assured him. "Although your friend was by, Mr. Laughton. I understand I should give his invitation to you. What was the earl's name?"

"Adam Darby," he said absently, reseating himself on the sofa as she took a chair across from him. Some part of him was pleased he'd followed her train of thought, but the rest of him was appalled by his behavior. His reaction to her innocent announcement had been as irrational as it was unnecessary. Joanna was surely safe in her own home. And Davis had checked on her. He did not need to worry.

And yet he couldn't seem to stop. When he held out the black velvet cloak to cover her bare shoulders above an amethyst silk gown, he thought how easy it would be for Daremier to strangle that graceful neck. Each time the carriage hit a rut, he tensed, wondering whether the axle had been tampered with and whether the carriage would suddenly pitch into the pavement. As they alighted at the theatre, he scanned the crowd for faces and saw an enemy in each smiling countenance. During intermission, the pop of a cork from a bottle of champagne sent him flying in front of Joanna to protect her from the gunshot. Her mother looked startled, and Joanna politely suggested that the older woman go see some friends in the opposite box. As soon as Lady Lindby left, Joanna turned to him.

"Is everything all right, Allister?" she asked. "You seem quite tense this evening."

She would have been an asset to the profession with that cool demeanor. Any other woman would surely be questioning his sanity.

"Forgive me," he replied. "I have a great deal on my mind."

"So I've noticed," she said. "My mother still needs a list from you of those you'd like to invite to the wedding."

He nodded, glad to have something normal to discuss. "Certainly. I'll drop it by tomorrow."

"Did you learn anything about that note?" she asked as if they discussed threats to her happiness every day.

So much for being able to avoid the subject. He managed a tight smile, though he found himself unable to meet her eyes for fear of the disappointment he would see there in his failure. "No. And I begin to think it is driving me mad."

Her hand covered his. "Don't let it drive a wedge between us. Can't you see that's what the villain wants?"

He brought his thumb up and rubbed the back of her hand, feeling the strength in those supple fingers. "All I see is that I may have put you in danger. I can't let that happen." He brought her hand up to his mouth and kissed it. He felt her shiver with pleasure.

"I see no reason to make a change in our lives for this," she murmured. "The danger does not trouble me overmuch."

Allister raised his head to meet her gaze, incredulous. "The danger doesn't trouble you? How can that be?"

She shrugged. "Perhaps because it's a part of who you are. I won't deny that it is a bit discomposing, but I think I can manage. I may not understand what you did for the War Office, Allister, but I can see it had a strong hand in shaping your life. I can also see that you miss it."

"You see a great deal," he told her, trying to keep his tone light. After years of keeping his thoughts private, it amazed him she could read him so easily. Perhaps it was time for him to retire, after all.

"Yes, I think I do," she replied. "Admit it, Allister. You miss the excitement of the chase."

"I suppose I do," he agreed. "My work has been central to my life for a long time. I will miss it, but I'm also tired of it. The days are long, Joanna, and the nights are empty. I think I will be content to sit at home and watch our children play at my feet."

"Will you?" she asked, dark eyes gleaming in challenge. "That seems a very narrow existence, my lord, for a man of your experiences."

He could not argue with her on that score. Yet, feeling her beside him, he thought perhaps he could make it work.

"There is something to be said for narrow existences," he told her. "They are predictable, safe. That is very appealing to me at the moment."

"Yes," she replied, returning her gaze to the stage as her mother rejoined them for the second act. "I can see how it might be appealing, for the moment."

Five

Joanna paced her room that night, calling herself six times a fool. How could she have been so blind? She'd feared she wasn't interesting enough for him. She had feared he didn't love her. Now she knew the situation was far worse. It wasn't so much he lacked in love but that he loved elsewhere. She had a rival, and she had no idea how to fight it.

She had heard of other women who had to fight for their husbands' attention. Racehorses, gambling, pugilistic displays, any and all of those things had been known to turn a man's head just as quickly as a lightskirt in front of Covent Garden. She had somehow thought that those wives were uninterested or unwilling to regain their places in their husbands' affections. She never thought to see herself take second place. She wouldn't do so now without a fight.

But how to fight? He claimed to want to settle down, but she was certain his desire for peace and tranquillity would not outlast the moment. She was just as certain that she was not interesting enough or beautiful enough to keep a man like Allister away from his other passion for long. What other weapons did she have?

The arrival of the mysterious note had given her a few days' grace before Allister discovered how truly uninteresting she was. The origin of the note clearly had him baffled. It was claiming his attention, and he was not unhappy about that. Yet she had complete confidence that he would eventually solve the mystery. Ten years of dangerous work would surely have given him the instincts and knowledge for self-preservation, at the least. It would also have honed his skills for solving problems like this one. He was on the hunt, and he would catch the culprit. Then she would be left with nothing but her staid little life to recommend her.

If only she could keep this level of excitement in their relationship. She had seen enough marriages to know that the ardor of courtship cooled quickly into a sedentary fondness in many cases. She had hoped that she and Allister might someday share a deeper bond. That hope was doomed unless she could find something that would entice him to stay with her. Unfortunately, she could not think of a thing.

She was still mulling over the matter the next day when Allister called. Elegant in his navy coat and fawn trousers, he brought her a nosegay of hothouse violets, brushing a kiss against her neck as he bent to give them to her.

"Thank you," she murmured, both for the flowers and the touch that filled her with longing.

"Oh, how lovely," her mother enthused. "My Joanna is fortunate in her choice of husbands."

Joanna was certain her smile was as strained as Allister's as he bowed over her mother's hand. She set the flowers into the lap of her lavender silk walking dress and tried to focus her attention on them.

"I'm the fortunate one, Lady Lindby," he assured her mother.

The flowers blurred out of focus as Joanna felt her

stomach knot. Surely there was some part of him that believed that statement. If only she could bring that part into the forefront, permanently.

"Yes, we do have a number of wedding gifts," her mother said in a characteristic non sequitur. "Since you're here, perhaps we should open a few."

"Madam, I am at your service," Allister replied with another bow.

Joanna could not help but smile at his kindness as her mother hurried from the room in a rustle of primrose silk to fetch the packages.

"You are very good to humor her," she told him as he stood waiting beside the sofa. She reached up and impulsively squeezed his hand. His warm gaze sent a ripple of heat through her.

"She's a dear woman," he replied. "Will she be all right when you come to live with me?"

Joanna swallowed the fear that that day would never come. "I'm sure she'll be fine. She has many friends, and I'll still visit frequently." Another thought struck. "Won't I?"

"Why wouldn't you?" he asked with a frown.

She let go of his hand. "I don't know. I merely wondered whether we'd be staying in London. We've never discussed where we'd live. Will your work take us far afield?"

He then sat beside her on the sofa, taking both her hands in his. "Joanna, I've retired. That note is the only reason I'm still working. I have a small estate in Somerset, near Wenwood Park. I assumed we'd go there for the summer and winter holidays and spend the rest of the time in London. But I'll live wherever you'll be happy. We can live on the moon for all I care."

"I don't think that will be necessary," she replied with

a smile. Why was it that one look from those deep blue eyes could send the worries flying from her mind, and another brought them crowding back? Before she could say more, her mother bustled back in, followed by their maid, footman, and butler, each carrying an armload of packages.

Joanna and Allister spent the next hour and a half opening presents. She was amazed and delighted with the variety and thoughtfulness of the gifts sent by friends and family. Aunt Seralyn had sent an ormolu clock that had belonged to their grandmother. Cousin Charles sent a papier-mâché box lined in velvet for her rings. Allister's cousin Justinian Darby, who studied literature at Oxford, sent a book of poetry.

"Love poetry," Allister said with a wicked grin. "Just the thing for cold winter nights."

Joanna wanted to return his teases, but her heart quailed. So many lovely gifts, so many heartfelt sentiments for her future. Would she have to send them all back?

At last all that remained was a single white box, about four inches square.

"Oh dear," her mother said with a frown. "We seem to have misplaced the card."

Joanna glanced at the pile of crumpled wrapping at their feet. "In all this mess, it's not surprising. Let me open it, Mother. Perhaps we'll know who sent it by the contents."

Her mother held out the box to her, but Allister neatly intercepted it.

"No, allow me," he insisted quietly.

Joanna frowned at him. "Is something wrong, Allister?"

His smile was once more strained, though she thought

someone else might not notice the tension. "No, not at all," he assured her. "I'd simply like to open this one. Would you mind?"

"No, of course not," she replied. She sat back, and he pulled the box to him. But, instead of opening it, he stood and carried it to the window.

"Allister?" Joanna asked.

"I need a little more light," he explained.

She exchanged glances with her mother. Lady Lindby shrugged indulgently, as if it were only to be expected for a prospective groom to act strangely. Joanna glanced back at Allister. He stood staring down at the box, brow wrinkled, as if he could hope to see the contents simply by staring hard enough. He must have caught her puzzled frown, for he turned his back on her. The faintest of ripples in his well-tailored coat told her he had flung off the lid. He stiffened. Before she could ask what it was, he whirled.

"This is from one of my relatives," he announced. "A personal gift. I'll acknowledge it myself. Were there any others, Lady Lindby?"

"No, that's the lot," her mother replied with a sigh of relief. "Though I expect to see quite a few more before the big day."

"I'd like to help open those as well," Allister told her. "It's very important to me to be part of these preparations."

Her mother blinked at his firm tone. "Well, certainly. You are the groom."

Something was wrong. Joanna could feel it. "Mother," she interrupted, "would it be all right if I had a few moments alone with Allister?"

Her mother rose gracefully. "Of course, dear. My

mother arranged my wedding once. I remember how it feels. Until tomorrow, my lord."

Allister bowed. "Good day, Lady Lindby."

As soon as her mother was out of the room, Joanna rounded on him. "What happened, Allister?" she demanded. "What's in that box?"

He glanced down at the relidded box as if surprised he still held it. "This? I told you, it is a personal gift from my family."

"I certainly hope you lied better than that when you worked in the War Office," Joanna informed him.

He raised an eyebrow. "My dear Joanna, whatever makes you think I'm lying?"

"Is it a game you want?" she demanded, fury rising at his unwillingness to be honest with her. "Very well, I can play this, I believe. I think you are lying, my lord, for several reasons. First, you didn't care about who opened what until we reached that box. Second, you have precious few family members and we've already opened the presents from the Darbys, so that excuse doesn't wash either. Third, I can feel the tension in you. Now, will you just confess so we can get on with this?"

He frowned. "I can see how you might have been misled. I wanted to open the package because I thought you might be tiring. And I have other family members outside the Darbys. I've told some of them about the wedding, so it isn't surprising they might want to send a gift before receiving the invitation. And the only tension you feel is embarrassment that I continually forget to give your mother the names of those family members so she can send an official announcement. You should have more faith in me, Joanna."

"No, Allister," she replied, stung. "You should have

more faith in me. I think it bodes little good for our marriage if you are hiding things from me."

He was silent for a moment. "Am I not allowed to protect you?" he asked quietly.

"Where I cannot do so myself, certainly. But I would like you to do me the courtesy of letting me determine when that is needed."

He nodded. "Very well."

"Good," she said, rising. She held out her hand. "Now, show me what's in the box, Allister."

Six

Allister held the box to his chest. His beautiful, courageous, headstrong bride-to-be gazed up at him in challenge. Every fiber of his being cried out to protect her.

"I'd rather not," he murmured.

She bristled.

"I'll simply tell you," he continued quickly. "It's a dead bug."

She blinked. "A dead bug?"

"Yes." He watched for her reaction, expecting cries of alarm, demands for smelling salts. She merely frowned.

"I don't understand. Why would someone send us a dead bug for our wedding?"

He shoved the box behind him. "I have no idea."

"Incredibly poor taste," she went on. "Quite tacky. One could almost take it as a bad omen. Oh!"

Her startled gaze met his, and he knew she had reached the same conclusion. He stepped to her side.

"Don't let it upset you," he cautioned. "Perhaps it's simply poor taste, as you said."

"Let me see it," she demanded. "And we'll see exactly how bad this taste is."

"I'd rather not," he repeated. "I'd like to take it to

the War Office, see if anyone there can make sense of it."

She paled. "You think it's from the one who wrote the note?"

"Possibly," he replied. "Let me handle this, Joanna. Just go about the wedding preparations as if nothing happened." He offered her an encouraging smile, but her gaze when it met his was implacable.

"Nothing has happened," she answered him. "I don't like this business, Allister, but I don't intend to let it come between us."

"That's my girl," he replied heartily.

Allister only wished he felt so confident as he took a hack back to the War Office that afternoon. In truth, finding the insect in the box had unnerved him. That Daremier could get so close to Joanna undetected was unthinkable. There had to be something he could do to stop the villain.

To his surprise, Lord Hastings had other ideas.

"You're not thinking clearly, my lad," his superior maintained when he proposed flushing out the French spy again. "You're entirely too involved."

"When have you known me to lack in judgment?" Allister countered. "You all keep saying I'm the best man you have. For God's sake, put me to work!"

Lord Hastings shook his head from where he sat behind the walnut desk. "You *were* the best man I had. Two things changed that. One—you retired. I know from experience that when a chap feels it's time to quit the Service, he's generally right. Two—you can't see beyond Joanna Lindby's pretty face. Sorry, Trevithan. Let the other fellows handle this one."

"But they aren't handling it," Allister declared. He yanked the box from his pocket and threw it on the desk. "Look at that."

Frowning, Hastings drew the box to him. He smoothed his palms down his bottle green coat, then carefully lifted the lid and peered in. His short nose wrinkled in obvious distaste.

"Nasty looking thing," he said. "Where'd you get it?"

"That was delivered to Joanna Lindby," Allister told him, "as a wedding present."

Hastings glanced up at him and back down at the insect. "I take it you see something evil in that?"

"Don't you?" Allister demanded. "A bug with a jeweled pin through its back? Doesn't that strike you as a rather menacing wedding present?"

"Strikes me as a damn queer wedding present," the marquis replied. He leaned back in his chair and eyed Allister. "However, it also strikes me as just the sort of creepy joke The Skull would pull."

"Exactly," Allister proclaimed. "If he can bring this to Joanna's house, she can't be safe."

Hastings stroked his mustache. "I could give her a bodyguard. Would that help?"

"Frankly, old man," Allister replied with relief, "I'd be indebted to you."

Hastings rose. "Good enough, then. I'll have someone at the house day and night. I take it you'll clear that with Lady Lindby and your intended?"

Allister paused. "Must I? I'd prefer they didn't know. I don't want to worry them."

"Dashed hard to protect someone who doesn't know she needs protecting," Hastings complained. "What do you want the fellows to do, loiter in the street? Won't that just tip off The Skull nicely?"

"You have a point," Allister acknowledged. He thought for a moment. Joanna had been through enough already. He hated to see her locked into having a strange man follow her about. But perhaps it didn't need to be a stranger. He met Hastings's frown.

"I have it. Davis can be your man during the day, and I'll watch at night."

"I already told you that you're disqualified," Hastings replied. "Besides, I can't imagine Lady Lindby liking having her future son-in-law staying the night. People will talk."

Before Allister could counter, there was a knock at the door. Hastings barked a command to enter, and Allister stepped aside and turned. The thick walnut door opened to admit Davis. Seeing Allister in front of the desk, he hesitated, then he squared the shoulders of his brown coat and moved into the room.

"Lord Hastings," he greeted with a bow. "Lord Trevithan. I didn't intend to interrupt."

"Quite timely, actually," their employer replied. "Seems The Skull has contacted Joanna Lindby."

"What!" Davis cried, rushing forward. "When? Where? Is she all right?"

Allister eyed his friend. After working with Davis for ten years, he knew his temper and responses well. Davis was cool under fire. Little rattled him. That he would so explode now could only mean something was up. Hastings must have wondered at the outburst as well, for he raised an eyebrow and leaned back in his chair again.

"Do you have something to contribute to this discussion, Mr. Laughton?" he asked.

Davis glanced between the two of them. He stood a

little taller. "Yes, sir, I do. I was making my usual rounds in London, checking my sources . . ."

"And how is that new opera dancer at the garden?" Hastings inquired dryly.

Davis had obviously regained his composure, for he did not so much as flinch. "Ready to do her duty for England, my lord. May I continue?"

"Certainly." Hastings waved him on expansively.

"Thank you. As I was saying, I checked my sources to see whether any of them had heard about The Skull being in England."

"And what did you learn?" Allister demanded.

Davis met his frustrated gaze. "Brace yourself, old man. He got in two days ago."

Allister stiffened. Some part of him had hoped he was wrong, that he'd somehow inflated the events of the last two days all out of proportion. But it was true. The Skull was in London.

He waited for the shiver of anticipation to snake down his spine as it usually did when he had to match wits with the arch spy. Instead, a heavy coldness settled in his chest.

Joanna was in danger.

He could lose her.

"Did you hear me, Trev?" Davis probed. "I said you were right—The Skull is in London. We must stop him before he acts."

"Bit late for that, I'm afraid," Hastings put in. He poked the box across his desk with a thick finger. "Look at this, Laughton. Tell me what you make of it."

Davis frowned, glancing into the box. Then he looked up, first at his employer and then at Allister, eyes clouded in obvious confusion.

"It appears to be a scarab beetle," he replied. "Late

Egyptian period, if I remember correctly from my studies at Oxford. Lord Elgin has several in his collection, as does Eugennia Welch. Someone steal one?"

Allister stepped forward to peer into the box even as Lord Hastings bent nearer as well.

"Egyptian, you say?" the marquis asked with a frown.

"In your opinion, Davy," Allister murmured, mind sifting through possibilities, "would someone give this as a wedding present?"

Davis shrugged. "Bit pricey and somewhat fussy, but I believe the creatures were considered good luck, so it is possible." He stiffened. "Good God, are you saying someone sent this to Miss Lindby?"

Allister nodded. "It was in with the other wedding gifts. There was no tag."

Davis pursed his lips. "And you think it was from The Skull?"

"It is rather like his usual tricks," Hastings reminded him. "Remember the funeral wreath he sent to Lord Michman the day before he assassinated the fellow? Devilish sense of humor. But if the ugly thing is valuable, it does seem less likely. Still want to go through with your bodyguard idea, Trevithan?"

Allister shook his head. "No, my lord. Given Mr. Laughton's report, I return to my earlier suggestion. We should try to capture the blackguard."

"Let's not start that again," Hastings grumbled. "I will not use you as bait."

"I agree," Davis put in even as Allister opened his mouth to protest. "Sorry, old man, but if you're right, I'm not sure you'd make such a good target. And I'd prefer to have you at my side."

"Then what do you suggest?" Allister asked.

"I think we should use something flashier."

"What would that be?" Hastings demanded.

"I suggest," Davis said, widening the distance between himself and Allister, "that the best bait would be Joanna Lindby."

Seven

Joanna puzzled over the strange gift the rest of the afternoon. She asked her mother about the matter, but Lady Lindby's mind was already working on place settings for the wedding breakfast and her answers were even more confused than her usual conversation. In the end, Joanna could only go about her business and hope that Allister had been wrong.

She had planned on a quiet night home with her mother and was surprised when their butler announced Allister. She was even more surprised to find that Lord Hastings and Davis Laughton were with him. Despite the late hour, all three were still dressed in their day clothes, dark coats and lighter trousers.

"My, how lovely," her mother proclaimed as they bowed in turn over her hand. "It's very good to see you again, Mr. Laughton. You must miss the country. And Lord Hastings. When was the last time I saw you? Did he win that boxing match?"

For once, Joanna was at a loss to translate. As Davis frowned and Allister grinned, Lord Hastings bowed again. "Your servant, Lady Lindby. Yes, we haven't seen each other since the day your late husband Jonathan joined me for the boxing match between Gentleman

Jackson and Mendoza. That was a day. Very sharp of you to remember."

Her mother beamed.

"To what do we owe the honor of this visit?" Joanna put in, hoping to bring the conversation back to something they all knew.

Davis and Allister exchanged glances. Hastings smiled at her mother. "Why, I'd heard you'd received some very interesting wedding gifts." He met Joanna's gaze, and she remembered the insect. "I wonder, Lady Lindby, would you be willing to show them to me? I'm sure we can trust these young people to entertain themselves."

Her mother agreed and happily led him off to the dining room, where they had piled the gifts on the sideboard. Davis went to close the door behind them.

"What is it?" Joanna hissed to Allister. "Has something happened?"

His jaw was hard, his eyes harder as he watched his friend return. "Mr. Laughton has a proposal for you. I don't like it above half, but I promised him I'd stand by your decision."

She frowned as Davis seated himself.

"Mr. Laughton?" she asked, indicating him to proceed.

"Miss Lindby," he began, just as serious as Allister, "what I'm about to tell you must be kept in strictest confidence. You cannot speak of it to another living soul outside those in this room, including your mother and your minister. I must have your promise on that before I continue. Do you agree?"

She glanced at Allister, who stared back at her, unmoving. This was it. She was about to learn all. Excitement mingled headily with fear. She swallowed both down and sat straighter. "I agree," she said firmly.

Allister closed his eyes as if in prayer, then reopened them. Davis nodded.

"Excellent," he said. "Miss Lindby, I'm sure you'll remember that I told you Lord Trevithan and I work for the War Office."

Allister stiffened again, frowning at him, but Davis did not pause.

"England has been at war for some time, and good men are needed," he said in careful explanation.

"I read the paper, Mr. Laughton," she informed him. "I am not uneducated in civil affairs."

"Of course," he replied graciously, but somehow she did not think he believed her. "You will understand, then, that in any military endeavor, there is that effort reported in the papers and that effort done in silence."

"The Secret Service," she murmured.

He glanced at Allister, who did not so much as nod in encouragement. She felt for him, but she had to know the truth.

"Yes, Miss Lindby, the Secret Service. Lord Trevithan has assisted the Service several times in the past, as have I and Lord Hastings."

She somehow thought assistance was the least of Allister's contributions, but she merely nodded as he continued.

"We have recently learned that a dangerous French agent known as The Skull may be in London. We believe he may be the one who has been threatening you."

"I see," Joanna replied. Despite her best effort, the fear was edging out the excitement. Something was wrong. The tension in Allister was not her imagination.

Were they sending him away or incarcerating him for his own safety?

"What do you want of me?" she asked with difficulty.

Davis glanced at Allister again, and she braced herself for the answer. Davis returned his dark gaze to her. "We'd like your help in catching him."

Joanna blinked. "My help?"

Allister leaned forward at last, laying a hand protectively on her shoulder. She relished the touch and his strength, for she didn't know how to respond.

"You don't have to put yourself in danger, my dear," he told her. "I told them this plan was unthinkable. A gently reared young lady is hardly the type to go against a master criminal."

Joanna stiffened. She should have been buoyed by his support, but his assessment stung. Did he think her a coward, or merely incapable?

"Certainly we will understand if you decline," Davis put in, watching her. "I cannot underestimate the danger. It takes a strong person to stand up to a devil like The Skull."

Joanna glanced between the two of them. Allister's eyes were stormy with emotion. He clearly did not want her to agree. Yet if she disagreed, would she not in effect have turned her back on his past, implied that she rejected it and him as well? And while she felt no need to endear herself to Davis Laughton, she could hear the challenge in his words. It would take a woman of strength to accept the challenge. Could any lesser woman hope to keep the heart of a man like Allister Fenwick?

"I told you this was a ridiculous idea," Allister said heatedly to his friend.

"Yes, well, it was worth a try," Davis maintained. "Sorry to have troubled you, Miss Lindby. I'll fetch His Lordship and—"

"I'll do it," Joanna interrupted before her courage could flee.

"What?" Allister cried, releasing her to collapse against the back of the sofa.

Davis stared at her. "Miss Laughton, are you sure?"

"Yes, I am," she said firmly, willing herself not to back down as Allister stared at her. "I want to help. Tell me what you need me to do."

"Joanna, you can't," Allister declared. "It's too dangerous!"

"May I remind you, Lord Trevithan," Davis said before Joanna could respond, "that you agreed to abide by Miss Lindby's decision?"

"Well, I jolly well never expected her to say yes!" Allister jumped to his feet and began to pace. "Do you have any idea how dangerous this could be, Joanna? No, of course you don't. Hang it all, Joanna, this man could kill you!"

Joanna shivered, but she forced herself to rise as well. "If he's that dangerous, then he could kill you, too. Do you think I like the idea of you in danger?"

He paused to eye her. "Probably no better than I like the idea of you in that situation."

"Precisely," she said, crossing to his side and peering up at him. "This man threatens us, threatens our future. Let me help you put a stop to it."

He traced the outline of her cheek with one finger. "You've left me with little choice. God help me, Joanna, I want to see this villain caught. But if anything should happen to you . . ."

She caught his hand and pressed a kiss into his palm. "Nothing will happen," she promised.

She thought for a moment he would continue to argue. Emotions danced across his face—anger, frustration, fear. But the one that touched her heart was the flash of pride, pride in her. He turned to eye his friend. "Very well, then. You have your answer, Mr. Laughton. Let's get this over with."

The next afternoon, Joanna found herself waiting in a closed carriage near a small pastry shop, just off St. James. Davis Laughton had somehow learned that the man known as The Skull had been seen buying bread there every afternoon for the last two days. They could only hope it was a pattern. She was to wait until he arrived, then go inside and make sure he knew who she was. She was then to find a way to leave and allow him to follow her. Davis, Allister, and Lord Hastings's men would do the rest.

Allister sat beside her, one arm draped protectively about her shoulders. Ever since he had come for her, she had sensed the change in him. Before, intrigue had seemed to flow from him like smoke from a tallow candle. Now, it was tension that coiled around him. She felt it ensnaring her as well. He was so certain she was endangering her life. Surely he knew more about these matters than she did. He'd lived in this kind of danger for ten years. What was she doing here?

He shifted in the seat so that he could see her face, and it was the most natural thing for her to lean against him. His lips brushed hers in a gentle kiss, promising untold pleasures. If this was her last moment in life, she wanted to savor it. She ran her hands down the soft wool of his navy coat, feeling the muscles that lay hidden beneath it. She breathed in, hoping to catch the scent of his cologne, something to help etch the moment in her mind. But she only smelled leather and damp wool and dry straw. Even Allister's scent was a secret. She sighed.

"It's not too late to change your mind," he murmured.

She shook her head and leaned back, hoping he hadn't felt her trembling. "No. I promised."

From outside came a sharp whistle. Allister stiffened. "That's the signal. Be careful, Joanna!"

She started for the door and fear seized her. What if she were killed? What if Allister were killed? She couldn't let this be their last moment before eternity. She whipped back and threw her arms about him, kissing him with all her heart. She felt his arms come around her, his cool lips grow warm beneath hers. A few moments ago he had kissed her gently. Now he took everything she offered. She gave herself up to the feelings of joy, delight, desire.

The shrill whistle repeated.

She broke away with difficulty. Allister caught her shoulders.

"To hell with the lot of them," he growled. "We'll run away—to Naples, to America. Don't go, Joanna. If anything happens to you, I'll never be whole again."

She could feel tears starting and blinked them forcefully away. Her plan was working. He had admitted he cared for her. She could not damage that fragile care by turning back now.

"It will be all right," she promised, praying to God that she spoke the truth. "Just remember: I love you." She pulled out of his grip and stepped from the carriage.

Eight

Joanna waited nervously in line in the little pastry shop. Somewhere in front of her, beyond the women and gentlemen waiting their turn, was The Skull. Once away from the narrow front window, it was amazing how dark the wood-paneled room became. She could barely make out the chubby baker behind the chest-high row of glass-front display cases and all she could see in front of her was the back of the fellow on whom he waited. She didn't have to see the jellied pastries and cakes and pies that rested temptingly in the cases—the sweet smell of sugar and spices permeated the shop. To her left, a gangly apprentice helped a tall, thin gentleman to a set of hot cross buns, steam still rising from them in a heady aroma. To her left a woman shifted a crying baby in her arms and pulled out a plump purse to pay another waiting apprentice.

From behind her came a giggle. Joanna did not have to turn to know it came from the woman from Lord Hastings's staff who was posing as her maid. The apprentice on her left was reddening, and Joanna would have bet the woman was flirting with him. Allister had explained that this supposedly flirtatious nature was an act to provide an easy excuse for her to lag behind and let the spy reach Joanna. At the moment, Joanna would rather the woman was an Amazon of legend, here to protect her. Her fashionable rose-striped spencer seemed to tighten around her ribs with each second. Her feet seemed to grow heavier inside the primrose day dress.

"Smile," the woman hissed behind her as they took another step toward the counter.

Now at last Joanna could see the man directly in front of the baker. A poke in her back told her this was their quarry. He accepted his package of bread and turned toward them. Joanna pasted on a smile and willed herself to gaze at the villain.

He was not nearly as fearsome as she had expected. Indeed, she would never have suspected him for a spy or any other kind of criminal. The man before her was wizened in his rumpled brown coat and trousers, his head bent so that all she could see easily was the brim of his top hat. One hand trembled as he held the bread; the other clutched a book of poetry to his chest. He appeared no more dangerous than a minister out for an afternoon stroll or a college don skipping class. Joanna blinked and disappointment shot through her. Was all this for nothing? Could they have been mistaken? Could this be a fool's errand?

The woman nudged her in the back again. There was no more time for questions. She took a deep breath, then stumbled, fetching up against him. The loaf of bread slid from his hand to bounce once on the flour-speckled wooden floor.

"Oh, pardon me," she gushed.

Black eyes gazed into hers, cold and fathomless. And absolutely without recognition. She blinked again, then smiled graciously, praying he could not hear the uneven cadence of her pulse.

"I'm terribly sorry," she said by way of explanation.

"I've been out shopping all day, and I'm afraid I'm tired. May I buy you another loaf of bread?"

"That would be very kind," he replied in a quiet, gentle, very English voice.

She nodded and motioned for her maid to step forward and do the deed. "Get this gentleman a loaf of bread, Maudie, and don't forget those sweet rolls Lord Trevithan is so fond of."

"Yes, mum," the supposed maid replied, scurrying around them. Joanna glanced at the man in time to see a look of speculation cross his dark gaze. Anticipation replaced the disappointment in her veins. This was almost like a game of chess, she saw suddenly. Move, countermove, position, counterposition. Her father had taught her to play when she was very young, but she liked to think she had gained some mastery of the game. Perhaps this adventure would not be any different.

"I suppose I'm going to have to find a cook who makes these rolls once we are married," she confided, smiling at him. "My fiancé Lord Trevithan can't seem to get enough of them. Ah, here we are."

The maid handed the man another loaf with a hurried curtsey, then turned back to Joanna. "And did you want to pick out the jellies for your wedding breakfast, mum?"

Joanna shook her head and laughed, fairly confident that only those who knew her well would hear how forced it sounded. "My word, where is my mind today? Thank you for reminding me, Maudie. Excuse me, sir."

He bowed and turned to leave. Joanna stepped up to the counter with mixed emotions. Had she been too obvious? Why didn't he make another move? Then she shook her head. His next move would be to attack her. Of course he could not do that in public. The woman with her baby was still being waited on by the young apprentice. The baker was waiting with a scowl to help her and Maudie. She had nothing to fear. She spoke confidently to the baker, asking after prices and how he managed deliveries. When he turned away to pick up another batch of pastries to show her, Maudie nudged her elbow.

"You're doing fine," she whispered to Joanna, who felt as if her limbs were about to turn to apricot jelly. "Now we see whether he takes the bait. Tell me to pay for this and start for the door."

She wanted more than anything to look back and see where the man had gone, but that would have given away the game. "That will be sufficient for now, sir," she said to the baker. "Pay the man, Maudie. I'll wait outside."

Turning, she scanned the dim room. Nowhere did she see The Skull, if that was who the little man really was. She still couldn't help wondering whether it was all a mistake. Of course, that was probably the part of her that didn't want to admit she was about to tempt a dangerous criminal to take her life. She made a show of flouncing to the door. When Maudie turned to nod to her, she swept out into the sunshine.

There she paused to blink in the sudden light. Ladies and dandies strolled past. On the street beyond, carriages and lorries vied for space. Street vendors trundled by, shouting the praises of their wares. It was all disgustingly normal. Joanna took a deep breath and forced her shoulders to relax.

"I believe I know your fiancé," The Skull said quietly beside her.

She jumped, then smiled stiffly, hand to her chest to cover the wild beating of her heart. "Really?" she asked, hoping she did not sound as startled as she felt. "Then perhaps you'd like to accompany me. He is to meet me just down the street to help pick out linens for our new home. I'm sure he'll be glad to see you."

He smiled sadly. "No, my dear, I'm afraid he won't."

What happened next was a blur. Something silver flashed in his hand, and Joanna only had enough time to blink before she was struck from the side and flattened into the building. She braced her fall with her hands, feeling the brick bite through her kid-skin gloves even as a powerful male shape pressed against her back. Around her, cries echoed and footsteps thudded. It would all have been quite alarming if she hadn't recognized the voice in her ear as Allister's.

"Don't move," he cautioned. "They nearly have him in hand."

"I wouldn't dream of moving," she replied, feeling his strong arms around her. Indeed, if the brick hadn't been pressed nearly to her nose, she might have enjoyed the touch of his body to hers. She closed her eyes and let her pulse slow to a lazy beat. He released her just as slowly.

"Are you all right?" he demanded as she righted herself. He put his hands on her shoulders and peered into her eyes as if suspecting she had somehow damaged her soul. Funny how she'd never noticed how tender those eyes could be. She could easily lose herself in their depths.

"I've never been better," she murmured.

Davis dashed up beside them. "We got him, Trev!" he crowed. "In the act. It's Newgate for certain, if not the rope."

Joanna felt chilled suddenly as the reality hit home. Someone had tried to kill her. Yet the little man she had spoken to had disappeared, and the street once more looked normal, save for the curious stares of passersby. It was as if her near brush with death had never been.

Allister was scowling at his friend. "Enough, Davis. I'm taking Joanna home."

Davis bowed, but he could not seem to contain his enthusiasm. "Yes, yes, of course," he chattered as he straightened. "Nice job, Miss Lindby. We may call you for the trial."

"You will not," Allister informed him icily. "She is out of this, as of now. I'll see you later at the Office."

He hustled Joanna away before she could say anything.

Once they were in the carriage, heading for Mayfair, he once more enfolded her in his arms. "What a nightmare," he said, cuddling her against his chest. "I'll wager you're glad it's over."

She hated to argue with him when she was in the most satisfactory position of his lap, but she couldn't stay silent. She had gone through with the deed to prove her valor; negating it now would spoil everything.

"Actually, I rather enjoyed it," she replied.

He pulled back to stare into her face. "Enjoyed it?"

She traced the paisley pattern on his waistcoat with her finger, suddenly embarrassed to admit it in the face of his surprise. "Yes, Allister, truly. I know that will seem strange to you, but there was a certain thrill knowing that I could best an infamous French spy, that every move and every word counted. It was very much like a game of chess."

"Not so strange," he murmured. "I've often thought of it as a game. That's the only way to stay sane sometimes. But the excitement can be a drug, Joanna. You can become addicted or worse, you can come to take the danger for granted and lose your life in the process."

She swallowed. "Well, neither of us has to worry about that. This is our last case."

He was silent and alarm rose in her. "Allister? This *is* our last case, is it not? We've caught your Skull. What more must be done?"

He pressed a kiss against her temple before answering. The sweet touch brought her no comfort. "I must go by the Office and interrogate him," he said soothingly. "Once I know he acted alone, I can be satisfied."

Somehow, Joanna was afraid neither of them would be satisfied.

Once Joanna was safely home, Allister hastened to the War Office. Every time he replayed the scene outside the pastry shop, he grew cold inside. He'd seen the flash of the knife. She had nearly been killed, would have been killed had he not leapt to push her aside. As he strode down the marble halls to Lord Hastings's office, his fists balled at his sides. The Skull would pay.

Davis glanced up from his questioning as Allister entered. Daremier sat calmly in a high-backed wooden chair, burly soldier on either side, a bored expression on his cadaverous face. Lord Hastings stood nearby, mouth set in grim lines. Davis hurried to Allister's side.

"You won't like this," he said without preamble.

"He had conspirators," Allister guessed, feeling his body chill all over again.

"Worse," Davis replied. "We can't hold him. He is completely innocent."

Nine

Allister stared at Davis. "Are you mad? Since when is threatening a woman with a knife innocent?"

Davis grimaced. "We thought we saw a knife, old chap. But we searched him thoroughly. He carried no weapon."

"So he threw it away, stuck it in a wall, passed it to a friend," Allister ranted. "Damn it, Davy, we can't let him get away again!"

"I told you you wouldn't like it," Davis replied. "We have no evidence he was armed."

"We all jolly well saw something flash in the light," Allister countered.

"What we saw," his friend said, "was apparently this." He handed Allister a slender silver case. Allister took it, watching it flash obligingly in the lamplight. Flipping open the lid, he found simple calling cards, black ink on embossed linen. He pulled out several, only to find that each bore a different name. The top card had a small hand-drawn skull in the corner.

"Quite a catch," Davis commented. "Several of the lads are chasing down those names. We know one belongs to a prominent eastside physician. Explains how the bugger slips in and out so easily. He has dual citizenship."

"And this isn't enough?" Allister demanded.

Davis shook his head. "Nothing illegal about using more than one name, Trev. And you know we have no witnesses to his earlier crimes—just supposition. In this case, apparently all he was going to do was give Joanna a calling card, the one with the skull on it. He says he merely wanted her to pass it on to you. The miscreant probably thought to shake you up a bit. Face it—the villain has us."

"I want to talk to him," Allister said.

Davis glanced over his shoulder to where Daremier sat with pursed lips. "Are you sure that's wise? You *are* a bit involved in this case, as His Lordship has pointed out."

Allister didn't repeat his request. He pushed past Davis to confront his enemy of so many years.

Daremier raised his head to meet his gaze. His black eyes sparkled with malevolent amusement; his thin lips curled in a sneer.

"Good afternoon, Baron Trevithan," he said in perfect English. "To what do I owe this pleasure?"

Allister glared down at him. Every other time he'd gotten close to the villain he'd been calm, cool, ready for the deadly game they played. Now his anger boiled within him, clouding his mind, hampering his reasoning. Some part of him recognized the problem and cautioned retreat. The rest of him cried out for blood.

He put his hands on the arms of the chair and bent to put his face within six inches of The Skull's.

"I want you," he spat out, "to stay away from Joanna Lindby."

Daremier didn't even blink. "Your charming fiancée? Certainly, my lord. And may I wish you every happiness."

"Don't wish me anything," Allister told him. "Don't come near me, don't even think about me. From now on, as far as you're concerned, me and mine cease to exist."

Daremier smiled. "I could only hope."

Allister's fists tightened on the arms of the chair. Lord Hastings stepped forward and laid a hand on his shoulder.

"That's enough, Trevithan. Let us carry on from here."

There was nothing left for him. He had no choice. The fact was totally unsatisfying. He forced himself to straighten. Daremier watched him.

"It would give me great pleasure to leave you with your doubts," the Frenchman said. "But I've enjoyed our association over the years. It's rare one meets a truly worthy gamesman. I offer you this gift to consider. If I am the spy you all think I am, why would I oppose your wedding? You obviously love this woman. Britain's most talented secret agent, safely married and raising a family? Unable to continue his work? Surely your enemies would only breathe a sigh of relief."

Allister stared at him, emotions warring. His instincts said the man was right, but how could he fully believe a spy who'd made a career of lying? Was there such a thing as honor among thieves?

"Come on, Trev," Davis urged at his elbow. "I'll walk you out."

Allister turned on his heel and left.

In the corridor, Davis pulled him up short. "Did you hear the arrogance? You can't let him get away with it, Trev! You can't leave the Service now. We've got to stop him."

Allister shook his head. "I'm done, Davy. This whole mess proves it. I've lost the knack."

"Nonsense," Davis argued. "You're just frustrated. The answer isn't to relax, it's to go after the bugger."

"My heart's not in it," Allister replied with a sigh. "I can't run the risk of anything happening to Joanna."

"It still could, you know," Davis reminded him. "Daremier denies sending the note or the scarab. But someone sent them."

Allister chilled. "You think he's lying? Or is there someone else?" When Davis did not answer, he ran his hand back through his hair in despair. "Curse it all, Davy, I'm a mess. Look at me—I can't think, I can't act. All I know is, if I lose Joanna, I might as well lose my life."

Davis regarded him fixedly, then he barked out a laugh. "Daremier is right. I don't know what it is about you, my lad, but I can't torture you either. I sent the note, Trev."

Allister started. "What?"

"I sent the note," Davis repeated, though he had the good sense to avoid Allister's outraged glare. "I had a friend write it so you wouldn't recognize the hand."

"Why?" Allister demanded. "What could you possibly hope to gain by it?"

Davis shrugged. "I knew you admired the chit, but I couldn't really believe it was love. I thought you were smarting over losing Daremier. I thought if you were presented with a mystery, you'd rise to the occasion. Instead, you just sank deeper. If this is love, old chap, it isn't very inspiring."

"On the contrary," Allister told him, "I find it quite illuminating." He cocked his head and eyed his partner. "I ought to plant you a facer, but instead I'll thank you. I wasn't sure whether I was running away or not. Now I know. It's love, Davy. She knows the truth about me, and she isn't afraid of it. In fact, I wonder whether she wouldn't make a better agent than I ever was. She's sharp and sweet and passionate. I can't imagine a life without her. The excitement, the adventure, none of this will be worth anything if it costs me Joanna. I'm done for, old man. I'm ready to live a normal life."

Davis nodded. "So I gathered. Which is why I must remind you of the scarab. Someone sent it, old chap. I know I didn't, and it looks as if Daremier didn't either. You haven't found our villain yet, Trev. You can't quit."

Joanna wanted so badly to unburden herself to her mother, but she knew she could not do so without giving the game away. Her mother had no idea of her involvement with the Service. She had been careful to make everything appear normal, telling her mother she was going out shopping with Allister for household items for their future home. But now that Allister had so much as admitted he was going to continue his dangerous work, she didn't know what to do.

She had lost. She had tried to show she could be part of his world, but still he shut her out. She had thought she had made progress for a time. Certainly his declaration in the carriage had warmed her heart. Yet he was not willing to leave the excitement behind. She could not compete with the Service after all. The villain had been caught—she had no mystery left to make her attractive. She had fought the battle and lost, and she had no other strategy to help her win the war.

Her mother's cheerful attitude did nothing to help. Lady Lindby bustled about the house, finishing the wedding preparations, chattering happily all the while. Joanna stitched slowly on her lace nightgown, wondering whether she would ever get to wear it. Her glance fell on the diamond ring again, glinting in the candle-light. It should be a symbol of their love. It was only a piece of stone, as cold as her heart. She was so lost in her misery that her mother had to speak twice before she realized she was being questioned.

"I'm sorry, Mother," she said. "I guess I was wool-gathering."

"That's to be expected, dear," her mother replied with a smile. "Lord Trevithan is a handsome fellow. And so considerate."

Joanna's smile was tight. "Yes, he is. What did you want to ask me?"

"Oh, nothing. I simply wanted to let you know I sent an acknowledgment to Eugennia Welch."

Joanna blinked. "Eugennia Welch?"

"Yes, dear. For that package. I must remember to tell Lord Trevithan that he was mistaken. The gift wasn't from his family, it was from your friend Miss Welch. She had it shipped all the way from that Egyptian ex-pedition she's sponsoring. Can you imagine?"

"No," Joanna managed. "I can't."

"I saw her companion, Miss Tindale, at the booksell-ers today when you were out. She asked after the pack-age. I can't understand how I could have gotten things so mixed up, but there you have it."

"You're sure?" Joanna pressed, mind whirling. "Mother, you're positive? Eugennia Welch sent us a dead insect?"

"Goodness, was that what it was?" Her mother raised her eyebrows in obvious surprise. "I knew your friend was a bit odd, but a dead insect? Why would she have to ship to Egypt for that? If she wished to give you a dead insect, she could certainly have found an English one for less trouble."

She continued on, but Joanna barely heard her. What did it mean? The insect had been an innocent gift, sent by an eccentric friend. What about the note? Was The Skull innocent after all? Was this a mystery she could use to her advantage?

Suddenly she froze. The devious direction of her thoughts appalled her. Was she truly willing to hold Allister by deceit, to keep him in a constant state of worry if that meant she kept him at her side? What had her doubts driven her to?

She had wondered why she had never met his friends. Now she knew he had been forced to rely on only a few intimates to stay alive. It was not that he was incapable of having friends, but that he had put his duty before the luxury. She had been afraid he would bore easily in their marriage and blamed him for that shortcoming. The problem was and always had been within her. She had to believe herself worthy of his love.

By the time Allister joined them that evening, she knew what she had to do. Allister had shown his true colors. It was time she showed hers. She would do something clever to show him she understood his life and to give him a chance to freely admit he loved her. If instead he rejected her, she would know this marriage was not meant to be.

It took little to get her mother to leave her alone with him. It took less to get him to talk about The Skull.

"I spoke with the villain," he admitted when she asked. "The result is not satisfactory."

Joanna swallowed. Though he did not seem pleased by the result, still she sensed a finality. He had come to a decision. "Then you will continue your work," she said.

He nodded. "I have little choice. However, I want you to know that one mystery has been solved. It appears that The Skull did not send the note. I am satisfied that the person who sent it poses no danger."

Joanna frowned at his insistence. "Then why do you persist?"

"That still leaves the gift," he explained. "There appears to be some reason to suspect that it is from a hostile source." He rose and went to stand opposite her. She tensed to hear his decision. He would tell her he meant to continue his work, that his duty would always come first.

When he spoke, the words were worse than she could have imagined. "Therefore," he said, "I have no choice but to postpone our wedding."

She had feared it was coming, but the verdict still stunned her. Her fingers tightened around each other in her lap, squeezing the diamond until it cut into her skin. He could be acting out of concern for her safety, or he could be acting out of a desire to continue his work. She almost told him the truth; that would have been easy. But if she did, she would never be certain of his love. She had to get him to see her for who she was, for what she offered. She had to follow through on her plan.

"I understand, Allister," she said quietly, reaching into the pocket of her gown. "And I think you should see this." She handed him a note. "It arrived this afternoon. The perpetrator asks you to meet at midnight tonight or our future happiness is in jeopardy."

Ten

"This is it, then," Davis hissed to Allister as they waited just outside the churchyard. "We've got men surrounding the place. Whoever is doing this won't get away this time."

"You'd better be right," Allister murmured, watching the dark shadows among the moonlit gravestones. "I can't take much more of this. You should have seen Joanna's face when I told her we had to postpone the wedding. I couldn't have hurt her more if I'd struck her."

"Surely she understands the necessity," Davis replied. "You are trying to save her life."

"She understands," Allister said. "She's too intelligent not to understand. Too brave as well. She wanted to come with me tonight."

Davis chuckled. "Pluck to the backbone, that one. You've found yourself a gem, Allister. Let's see what we can do to make sure you keep her."

"Hssst." The sharp sound brought them both to the alert. A moment later and a climbing boy darted into their hiding place in the alley.

"Look lively, me lords," he proclaimed in an excited whisper. "Someone's entered the churchyard from the High Street side. 'Is Lordship says go."

Allister nodded, moving easily out of the alley toward the cemetery. How many times had he done this over the years, crossed the space knowing he might meet his doom? It could have been a dinner party for the Duke of Milan, the fall threshing in Normandy, a crowded tavern in Portsmouth. The place or occasion didn't matter. In fact, they all tended to run together. Only this time was different.

This time was for Joanna.

He slipped through the wrought iron gate, giving it an extra push to make sure it squeaked loudly enough to be heard by the occupants, living and dead. He strolled casually through the tombstones and monuments, every sense alert. The faintest of breezes set the trees to rustling and caressed his cheek. A cat darted away from his approach. He could smell the musty odor of fresh-turned earth.

There was a cloaked figure awaiting him in the shadow of the church's cross. There was no answering rush in his blood. He felt only determination as he approached it. Tonight the game would end, one way or the other. He would not return from this churchyard without knowing Joanna was safe.

He stopped within five feet of the creature and bowed, keeping his eyes trained on the slender figure. His mind sorted through faces and physiques of his adversaries, trying to find a match.

"Good evening," he said. "As you can see, I've come as you asked."

"Are you alone?" the figure rasped out.

Allister frowned. He should know that voice. It surely belonged to a woman, though it was deepened and rough-edged. He decided not to lie, evading the question instead.

"Shall we get down to it?" he asked. "What do you want of me?"

His enemy paused, then raised gloved hands to lower the hood. Black hair glinted in the pale moonlight.

"Good evening, Allister," Joanna murmured. "What I want is your love."

She watched as Allister recoiled, face paling.

"Joanna! Do you have any idea how dangerous this is?" He strode forward and pulled the hood back over her hair. "I told you not to come. We have to get out of here before the villain arrives."

She pulled away from his outstretched arm, wanting only to feel it about her. "The villain has arrived, Allister. I wrote that note."

He stared at her. "Impossible. I swear I'd know your hand."

"Very well. I had the footman write it. And it cost me most of my pin money, and a promise in writing that he wouldn't be sacked if you found out."

"I don't understand." He frowned. "You knew I wanted to catch the miscreant who sent that insect. Why would you want to hinder that?"

"My friend Eugennia Welch sent that insect," she informed him. "Mother talked to her companion this afternoon while we were catching The Skull."

"Why didn't you tell me?" he demanded. "Why did you put me through all this?"

She peered closer. His color had returned; indeed, it had heightened. His blue eyes snapped fire and his powerful body towered over her. "What exactly did I put you through, Allister? I was under the impression you enjoyed this sort of thing."

"Enjoy it? Are you mad?" He ran a hand back through his hair. "I've been worried sick since the moment that first note appeared. I can't concentrate, I certainly can't track a criminal. For the first time in my life, I want out of the Service. This is no longer a game, Joanna. This is real. And it scares the life out of me."

She felt tears threatening. "I'm sorry to have caused you pain, Allister. But part of me is glad you care enough to be pained."

"Did you doubt that?" He watched her face and saw a pain mirroring his own cross her lovely features. "Yes, I can see you did. Forgive me, Joanna. I should have been more honest with my feelings. I've admired you from the first, but in truth, when I offered, I wasn't in love."

"I understand," she said, choking on the last word. "Your work is very important to you, to the nation. I was a fool to think I could compete with that."

He stepped closer and caught one of the tears that ran down her cheeks. "Yes, you were," he murmured. "There is no comparison. Nothing, no one, could hold a candle to you, Joanna. I love you with all my heart."

Her head jerked up; her eyes searched his face for confirmation. What she saw filled her with joy. With a glad cry, she threw herself into his arms.

Allister kissed her deeply, glorying in the feel of her pressed against him. He could imagine no more finer thing than this—to hold the woman he loved in his embrace. Joanna put all of herself into the kiss, her joy unbounded as she felt her passion returned. His arms tightened around her and his breath came as quickly as her own. Any doubts she might have had fled into the darkness. She could feel his love in every fiber of her being.

As if from far away, she heard movement among the tombstones. Allister raised his head. She could see the tender light once more shining from his eyes. His smile was just as sweet.

"Brace yourself, my dear," he murmured. "We have company." She stiffened as he raised his voice. "Hold your fire. I have the villain well in hand."

Davis stepped into the moonlight. "I can see that, old fellow," he quipped. "Interesting technique. I generally don't think to kiss them into submission."

Chuckles echoed around them, as if all the gravestones were laughing. Joanna reddened.

"I thought you were alone!" she accused.

His chuckle was for her alone. "I thought you were a villain. I promise never to be untruthful with you again, my love."

Joanna hugged the word to her heart as Davis joined them.

"So, how effective is that technique?" he teased Allister.

"I wouldn't recommend it," Allister replied coolly. "It has a tendency to fail. You see, while I have captured Miss Lindby, she has captured my heart."

"And what about your villain?" Davis demanded. "I suppose we have to come back another night for him."

Allister and Joanna exchanged glances. Davis stiffened.

"Do you wish to tell him or shall I?" Allister asked.

In his arms, Joanna knew there was nothing she could not do. "I wrote the note, Mr. Laughton," she admitted. "I should have thought Allister might ask the rest of you along. I'm sorry for the trouble. You see, at the time, I thought it was necessary."

"I share the blame," Allister put in before Davis could answer. "If I had been attending to my marriage instead of my duty, this would never have happened."

"Then there was no conspiracy?" Davis sounded only the slightest bit disappointed. "You really will be leaving us?"

"Yes, Mr. Laughton," Allister replied, with no regrets whatsoever. "I'm pleased to say you will no longer have need of my services. I intend to spend the rest of my life keeping Lady Trevithan out of trouble."

"That's right," Joanna agreed, giving him a squeeze. "And you'll need to start immediately, because we shall be married."

"In June," Allister completed.

And they were.

More Zebra Regency Romances

Put a Little Romance in Your Life With
Constance O'Day-Flannery

__**Bewitched** $5.99US/$7.50CAN
  0-8217-6126-9

__**The Gift** $5.99US/$7.50CAN
  0-8217-5916-7

__**Once in a Lifetime** $5.99US/$7.50CAN
  0-8217-5918-3

__**Second Chances** $5.99US/$7.50CAN
  0-8217-5917-5

—**This Time Forever** $5.99US/$7.50CAN
  0-8217-5964-7

__**Time-Kept Promises** $5.99US/$7.50CAN
  0-8217-5963-9

__**Time-Kissed Destiny** $5.99US/$7.50CAN
  0-8217-5962-0

__**Timeless Passion** $5.99US/$7.50CAN
  0-8217-5959-0

Call toll free **1-888-345-BOOK** to order by phone, use this coupon to order by mail, or order online at **www.kensingtonbooks.com**.

Name _____

Address _____

City_____ State _____ Zip _____

Please send me the books I have checked above.

I am enclosing $_____

Plus postage and handling* $_____

Sales tax (in New York and Tennessee only) $_____

Total amount enclosed $_____

*Add $2.50 for the first book and $.50 for each additional book.

Send check or money order (no cash or CODs) to:

Kensington Publishing Corp., Dept C.O., 850 Third Avenue, 16th Floor, New York, NY 10022

Prices and numbers subject to change without notice.

All orders subject to availability.

Visit our website at **www.kensingtonbooks.com**.

Merlin's Legacy

A Series From
Quinn Taylor Evans

Call toll free **1-888-345-BOOK** to order by phone or use this coupon to order by mail.

Name _____

Address _____

City _____ State _____ Zip _____

Please send me the books I have checked above.

I am enclosing $_____

Plus postage and handling* $_____

Sales tax (in New York and Tennessee) $_____

Total amount enclosed $_____

*Add $2.50 for the first book and $.50 for each additional book.

Send check or money order (no cash or CODs) to:

Kensington Publishing Corp., 850 Third Avenue, New York, NY 10022

Prices and Numbers subject to change without notice.

All orders subject to availability.

Check out our website at **www.kensingtonbooks.com**